The Garden of Earthly Delights

A JOHN WESLEY O'TOOLE NOVEL

ALSO BY WILLIAM RAWLINGS

PUBLISHED BY MERCER UNIVERSITY PRESS

Crypto (2023)
(A John Wesley O'Toole Novel)

The Columbus Stocking Strangler (2022)

Lighthouses of the Georgia Coast (2021)

Six Inches Deeper (2020)

The Girl with Kaleidoscope Eyes (2019)
(A John Wesley O'Toole Novel)

The Strange Journey of the Confederate Constitution (2017)

The Second Coming of the Invisible Empire (2016)

A Killing on Ring Jaw Bluff (2013)

PREVIOUSLY PUBLISHED

The Mile High Club (2009)

Crossword (2006)

The Tate Revenge (2005)

The Rutherford Cipher (2004)

The Lazard Legacy (2003)

The Garden of Earthly Delights

A JOHN WESLEY O'TOOLE NOVEL

William Rawlings

MERCER UNIVERSITY PRESS
Macon, Georgia

MUP/ P699

Published by Mercer University Press
1501 Mercer University Drive
Macon, Georgia 31207

28 27 26 25 24 5 4 3 2 1

Books published by Mercer University Press are printed on acid-free paper that meets the requirements of the American National Standard for Information Sciences—Permanence of Paper for Printed Library Materials.

Printed and bound in the United States.

This book is set in Adobe Garamond.

Cover/jacket design by Burt&Burt.

ISBN 978-0-88146-942-4 (Print)
978-0-88146-943-1 (eBook)
Cataloging-in-Publication Data is available from the Library of Congress

AUTHOR'S PREFACE

In *The Garden of Earthly Delights*, John Wesley O'Toole, a disbarred attorney-turned-art-dealer, continues with his efforts to return his life to some sense of normalcy, this time with his decision to ask his girlfriend, Jenna, to marry him. Jenna, like O'Toole, has her own sketchy past which she is trying to overcome while building a new future for herself and her young son. As so often happens with the best of intentions, O'Toole's plans go awry when Jenna is forcefully reminded of her former best friend, Mindy, who disappeared without a trace years earlier. After Mindy's remains are discovered in a shallow grave in rural south Georgia, it becomes evident that O'Toole's hopes for his and Jenna's future must be put on hold until the truth surrounding Mindy's death is known. The hunt for Mindy's killer rips open the shadowy world of Jenna's and Mindy's pasts, and with it a list of possible suspects, leading to a shocking and unexpected conclusion.

This is the third in the John Wesley O'Toole mystery series, following *The Girl with Kaleidoscope Eyes*, and *Crypto*. Like all works in this series, *The Garden of Earthly Delights* is written as a stand-alone novel. It is not necessary to have read others to appreciate this tale of mystery and suspense. John O'Toole is a fascinating, if imperfect, character and episodes from his unpredictable life will continue to appear in subsequent novels.

MERCER UNIVERSITY PRESS

Endowed by

TOM WATSON BROWN

and

THE WATSON-BROWN FOUNDATION, INC.

PROLOGUE

Sometimes during the course of life, it becomes necessary to change direction. For months I had been brooding about it. It was a difficult and deeply personal decision, one only I could make. Yet in doing so, in choosing a path forward, I would be setting course on a journey that I believed would change my world for the better and hopefully help restore some of what I had lost. If it had involved only me, the choice would have been a simple one, but it was intertwined with and totally dependent upon someone else, a person I had come to love. So, on an unusually chilly night in mid-February, I sat on the open porch of my apartment, bundled up in a down-filled jacket, staring at the few visible stars in the southern sky. Once again, for what seemed like the thousandth time, the options paraded through my thoughts. As if a sign from above, the siren of a passing ambulance reached a crescendo before drifting away into the night. "I'll do it," I said aloud to no one. "I'll ask Jenna to marry me."

With that issue settled, I moved on to the how and when and where. This would be—assuming she accepted my proposal—the second marriage for both of us. In some ways our histories were similar. In each of our situations, but for totally different reasons, our lives had spiraled out of control as our marriages imploded and the world collapsed around us. For me it had been the two years I spent in prison for a vehicular homicide charge, accompanied by the loss of my family and my license to practice law. For Jenna it was drugs, methamphetamine to be exact, the details of which we had never discussed.

We met by chance, initially at a court-mandated Narcotics Anonymous meeting, first becoming friends and later sometimes lovers as we struggled to return some semblance of order to our lives. Though we set no boundaries, we never discussed the past, only the present and the future. There were many things—events, situations, emotional and psychological trauma—that Jenna did not know about me, and I was certain there were an equal number of things that I did not know about her. Yet, the person whom I had first met that night was, to me, beautiful, both spiritually and physically. I wanted to spend the rest of my life with her.

CHAPTER 1

For a change, I was happy. Business at the gallery had been exceptionally good over the holiday season, with December and January sales exceeding any previous months since I took over management following my grandmother's death. It would have been great to be able to attribute this to the quality of the art works I had for sale, or perhaps my prowess at marketing, but deep down I realized that it was curiosity that initially drew many potential buyers to the shop, located on the ground floor of my grandparents' former home on Savannah's Liberty Street. Through no fault of my own, I had been somewhat peripherally involved in a couple of high-profile criminal cases since my return to the city after my release from prison. I had been aptly described in the press as "a local art dealer." Sometimes any publicity is valuable.

I was seeing Jenna frequently, though she had no idea of my plans to ask her to marry me. I wanted it to be both a surprise and something unique that she would fondly remember forever. Although she would not have taken the credit if offered, in many ways I felt that I owed her my life. After the betrayal and shooting death of someone I thought I could trust, I was devastated, a psychological wreck. Jenna had put her life on hold to help nurse me back to health. Without her love and support, I don't know what I would have done. I only knew that I wanted to be with her.

One of the consequences of the bountiful sales season was the depletion of my inventory. Graphic art—paintings, serigraphs, prints and the like—are not commodities. Like the collectors and decorators who purchase them, each is different, and must justify in the buyer's mind the often-significant cost of an object with no practical use other than adorning a wall or brightening a room. Unlike most retail establishments, one cannot simply call up a wholesaler and order a dozen quality canvases that appeal to style's latest fad. To fill our sales inventory for the coming months, I needed several dozen works on canvas, both large and small, plus a selection of serigraphs and perhaps a small sculpture or two. The one bright spot was the fact that the post-Holiday months are traditionally times of slow sales. Because of this, during the first half of the year there are a number of art fairs in major cities around the world, events where dealers bring works to sell to other dealers or galleries, artists attempt to convince galleries to showcase their work, and the public is given an opportunity to purchase art from a vast bazaar of offerings. Our sales through the end of the year had left me with an excellent surplus in the gallery's bank account. Thinking of Jenna, I came up with a plan.

During my previous life as an attorney and partner at the Atlanta law firm of Flagler, Zahn & Wynne, my specialty had been environmental law. It was not something that I had intended to do, but rather evolved after I joined the firm. During those years, I would normally attend two or three environmental conferences per year, in part to keep up with current trends and challenges, and in part to do some face-to-face marketing with the environmental rights community. On two occasions I spent a week or so in Madrid, Spain, for United Nations-sponsored conferences on environmental change. It is a beautiful city, with parks and plazas, world famous museums, great food, superb wines and a relaxed atmosphere that immediately made the visits there one of the highlights of my year.

Shortly after making the decision to ask Jenna to marry me, I was thumbing through a trade journal for art dealers when I spied a quarter-page notice advertising the upcoming ART-Madrid, Madrid's annual art fair, to be held in late April. I thought of the city, of its moods, of its romance, and of Jenna. The flowers would be in bloom. The weather would be delightful. It would be the perfect place to ask her to marry me. Now, all I had to do was work out the details.

First, I checked with Hattie, the gallery's long-term bookkeeper and financial voice of reason. "The gallery is in the best shape it's ever been. You've done a fantastic job, John, taking over things and building the business. Sure, a buying trip to Madrid will be pricey, but now you can afford it."

"How about someone to help me, an assistant? Would that be too much?"

"I think not," Hattie replied, smiling. "I suspect Jenna's never been to Europe." She had read my mind. I smiled back. "And her expenses would be a legitimate tax deduction as well," she continued.

"But please don't say anything to her or anyone else. I haven't asked her just yet. I want this to be a surprise."

"I won't. I promise," Hattie said, "but you've got to think about your one employee, too. I believe you might want to give Jessica a raise, or at the very least, a good bonus. She deserves it and we can afford it now." I asked her to decide what would be appropriate.

With Hattie's approval and financial endorsement, my next step would be to ask Jenna to come along as my assistant, disguising my true purpose. I shut the door to my office and called her at work. "Hey!" she answered, sounding pleased to hear my voice. "What a nice surprise. You never call me at work."

"I know, but this is business." I tried to sound serious.

"Oh...."

"I wanted to ask you to do something for me," I said, dispensing with the usual chitchat.

"And what's that...?"

"I'd like you to be my assistant...."

"Oh, John, you know I can't do that," she interrupted. "I have a great job now, and I can't drive to Savannah...."

I cut her off. "Let me finish, please." I paused for a few seconds. "I would like you to be my assistant on a buying trip. It will be in April."

"Oh," Jenna said again, her voice neutral. "Tell me more."

"I need to purchase inventory for the gallery. You know we've had a great year, and I'm low on things to sell. It would be good to have someone come along with me, to help me decide what to buy. You have a great eye for art...."

"I took several classes in art history in college." She told me something I didn't know.

"All the better. We'd be away for about a week or so." Jenna listened silently. "And it would be a chance to spend time together," I continued.

"The idea sounds good, but I have work, and my son, and...."

"I know we can work all that out."

"Okay, can you give me a few more details? I need to think about this...."

"I want to attend an art fair—I don't have the exact dates in front of me, but it would be the last week in April, a couple of months from now."

"And where, exactly? I hope it's not Atlanta. New York would be great. Or New Orleans—I've never been there. Or...."

"Madrid."

Jenna was suddenly silent, then, "Madrid? As in Spain?"

"Yes."

"Are you serious? You want me to go with you?"

"Yes."

Another moment of silence, then "You're not kidding are you, John? Please tell me you're serious."

"Yes, I am totally serious. There is an annual art fair in Madrid that attracts galleries, dealers and artists from all over Europe. I need to buy a number of works for the gallery's inventory and that would be a great place to pick them up."

"But it's in Europe...," she began.

"Bigger and better selection as far as I'm concerned."

"But what about my son, my job...."

"We can work it out, I'm sure. It's only for about a week."

"....and I'll need to get a passport, won't I? I've never been to Europe, and I don't speak Spanish and...," Jenna continued speaking over my replies.

"Hey!" I said, and she was suddenly silent.

"Again, we can work all that out. You'll have plenty of time to get a passport before we leave. And a lot of people in Europe speak English these days, especially in hotels and restaurants, so that's not a problem. We'd only need about two days of shopping at the fair. We can spend the rest of the time seeing the city, doing a bit of traveling....

"Oh, god, John. Please tell me again that you're serious. Please...."

“I am serious, and I honestly would like you to help me choose works of art to purchase for the gallery.”

“Yes, yes, yes, yes…, I would love to go. I grew up in Claxton, Georgia. I’ve never been out of the country. And the best part is that I would be with you, to show me things, to explore the city together, to….”

“Good,” I said. “You make me happy. Let me do some checking and I’ll call you tomorrow with some details.”

I put my phone down on the desk, realizing that within a few short minutes my world had become a better place.

CHAPTER 2

There was a lot I needed to do to make all this happen. Jenna had to get her passport, and probably had no idea where to start. I needed to register for the art fair as a gallery owner, make hotel reservations, look for flights to Madrid, and check off a seemingly endless list of small details. I needed an engagement ring. And most importantly, being the somewhat compulsive person that I am, I wanted to decide exactly when and where I would surprise her with my proposal. Jenna called shortly before ten the next morning with the good news that her employer had no problem with her taking an extra week of vacation for "such a wonderful opportunity," as he put it. The thought flashed through my mind that besides Jenna, very few people in Claxton had been offered a chance to visit Spain for a few days. Her parents had gladly agreed to keep her son while we were gone. Everything was falling into place.

I told Jenna that she needed to apply for her passport right away to be sure it arrived in plenty of time for our trip. Registering for the fair was as simple as filling out some online forms. I booked our plane tickets on Delta, splurging to buy seats in the former business class, now known under the ritzy name of Premium Select. After an hour or so of looking at options on the internet, I settled on booking a room at Madrid's relatively new Four Seasons hotel in the heart of the city near restaurants, shopping and other attractions. The art fair venue would be only a relatively short Uber ride away.

Finding a ring worried me. I had no idea what Jenna would like, or not like, or if she even wanted a ring or other token of my proposal. Should it be something simple that she could wear every day, or something more substantial? Since I was keeping my plans private, I didn't want to ask advice from Jessica or Hattie or anyone else. Then it occurred to me—my grandmother's jewelry. It was in a safe deposit box at the bank, and like the grand house I had inherited on her death, it simply had not been part of my world after my release from prison. Other than a perfunctory glance to satisfy her executor when I took over her estate, I had never examined it.

At 9:00 a.m. the next morning, I was waiting as one of the tellers opened the bank's front door. After showing my identification and handing my key to the attendant, I was ushered into the vault. The locker that had been leased by my grandparents was stuffed with old deeds, insurance policies, and other detritus of a fifty-plus year marriage, now only a memory. A simple rosewood jewelry box was filled with gold and silver bracelets, pearl earrings, and other finery which included an assortment of rings, most in yellow or white gold, some plain and others set with stones of varying color. This was all mine, inherited with my grandparents' deaths, but it symbolized the life I had been denied, and subsequently the life I had rejected. Picking through the rings I chose a yellow gold band with what appeared to be a diamond solitaire set off by blue sapphire baguettes on either side. It looked like it would fit Jenna's hand. We could have the size adjusted later if needed. Rummaging through the box, I found a small soft red leather drawstring pouch. I slipped the ring inside and placed it in my pocket. Now all was in place. The only thing I needed to do was decide exactly when to ask Jenna to marry me.

February became March, as the azaleas—and pollen—burst into bloom. It was Jenna's birthday. We celebrated the night with a quiet dinner at a Savannah restaurant and were back at my apartment long before midnight. I casually mentioned that maybe I needed a bigger place, and had been considering moving across the courtyard to my grandparents' former home. "It's yours, John," she said. "Why not? It's a wonderful place. All you're doing with it now is paying taxes and utilities and insurance while you hide here in this apartment in the back yard. This is your safe space, I know, but things seem to be going well now. Isn't it time to be yourself?"

I didn't reply, nodding acknowledgment. She was right, of course. My past aside, if we married, that would thrust me back into the mainstream. We would have a new life together, and though we had never discussed it, it still might be possible to have a child—or two—together. I mentioned, casually of course, that right now there was just me. Maybe one day if I had a family.... I didn't say more. Jenna gave a little laugh.

Jenna's passport arrived in a matter of weeks. I added the information to our bookings on the Delta website. We were flying from Atlanta to Madrid with a short layover in Amsterdam, but had a nonstop flight back. With only three weeks before our departure, I still had not decided how I wanted to ask for her hand.

I began studying the art fair's website and online catalogue, reviewing the galleries, dealers and artists scheduled to be there, trying to get a feel for what might be available and correlate it with the Savannah art market. It was no simple task, but rather sophisticated guesswork. Restocking inventory would be expensive, and if it didn't sell, I'd likely be stuck with it.

Taking a break, I decided to see what special events were scheduled to happen in Madrid during our stay there. If we spent two or three days at the art fair, we would have ample time to explore Madrid and perhaps take a day trip by train to Avila, or Segovia or Toledo. There were several food festivals around the city, and the major museums each had ongoing exhibitions. I had known Jenna graduated from Georgia Southern University with a major in Business Administration. I did not know she had an interest in more than a passing interest in art until she told me as I was asking her to accompany me on this trip. Perhaps she would like to spend more time in Madrid's museums. I made a mental note to ask her, and started taking a closer look to see what she might find appealing.

After a bit of reading and research, it seemed that most reviewers agreed that among the many museums in the city, the top three were The Prado, the Reina Sofia, and the unpronounceable Thyssen-Bornemisza, all within a pleasant walking distance from our hotel. The latter—most commonly known as the Thyssen—has an eclectic collection of nineteenth and twentieth century European and American art. The Reina Sofia is relatively new, opening in the early 1990s and specializing in twentieth century art. The greatest of them all is the Prado, whose collections rival those of any of the world's grand museums. Founded more than two hundred years ago, its collections include works by El Greco, Rubens, Velázquez, Caravaggio, Dürer, Bosch, and many others of equal fame. As I went from review to review and website to website, it suddenly struck me that the galleries of the Prado, surrounded by the eternal beauty and timeless romance of art, would be the perfect place to propose to Jenna.

Still online, I accessed the website of the Museo del Prado and began scrolling through images of the collections. There are thousands of paintings and other works of art in the museum's holdings, but it appeared that only the best or perhaps best known were featured. Many, most even, dated from the late Middle Ages through the nineteenth century. Religious themes were common, with dozens of depictions of the struggles of various saints, or the Annunciation of the Virgin, or of God and his Heavenly Host and similar. Not exactly romantic; not at all the atmosphere to make a life-changing decision. I wanted this to be a joyous occasion, the offer of a commitment based on love and future happiness for us both. I couldn't see my asking Jenna to marry me while standing in front of Caravaggio's *The Agony of St. Ursula*.

And then I saw the museum's collection of the works of the Dutch painter, Hieronymus Bosch. There are more than a dozen, about half attributed to the artist himself; the others less certain but in his style. The most famous of Bosch's works, named by later historians *The Garden of Earthly Delights*, was thought to have been painted around the year 1500. It is a huge triptych, a mysterious, phantasmagorical three-panel painting that depicts in the left panel the story of the Garden of Eden, in the much larger central panel a joyous celebration of the pleasures of life, and in a smaller right panel a vision of Hell. As I recalled from my self-taught art education in preparation to taking over the gallery, scholars over the years have offered varying interpretations of the hidden meanings of this painting, the exact nature of which was not recorded during Bosch's lifetime. One modern reviewer described it as a representation of "fleshy pleasure," referring to "a group of nude figures [who] intertwine while nibbling on a gargantuan, succulent strawberry. Others swing rapturously from palaces built of forms resembling turgid reproductive organs, shimmering crystals, and seed pods ready to burst. Fountains of clear blue water flow directly into mouths; fruits are plucked; and duos caress inside glistening bubbles, ajar open clam shells, and plump nectarines."[1]

This was it. It was in the presence of this painting, hopefully a graphic expression of joy and happiness and how I wanted our lives to be, that I planned to pledge my undying love to Jenna.

---

[1] *https://www.artsy.net/article/artsy-editorial-decoding-boschs-wild-whimsical-garden-earthly-delights"* Alexxa Gotthardt, Oct 18, 2019 (Accessed 3/25/23)

CHAPTER 3

The time flew by. I was talking to Jenna every day now, frequently answering silly little questions about the upcoming trip, assuring her that the basics of life in Spain were not that different from those in Savannah, and that she need not worry about her inability to speak Spanish. I contacted my ex-wife's lawyer to say that I would be out of the country for a few days. He sounded reasonably pleasant—for a change—and said he'd pass the message on. Even though I'd be away only about a week, Jessica and Hattie scurried about making sure I'd prepaid all the bills and answered any pending questions. I pointed out that my phone worked as well in Madrid as it did in Savannah, to which Jessica replied, "But you'll be four thousand miles away…."

On the day of our departure, a Friday, we left Savannah late morning to catch our afternoon flight out of Atlanta, with a scheduled arrival about midday on Saturday in Madrid. Jenna was giddy, but calmed down a bit after settling into our seats and having a glass of champagne. The flight, including our brief layover in the Netherlands, was unremarkable. We both slept fairly well, and cleared immigration and customs in Madrid without a hitch. Less than an hour later we were settled into our room at the Four Seasons Hotel on the Calle de Sevilla in the heart of the city. The weather was balmy, with a blue sky and fluffy white clouds. The art fair began on Monday, so we had the remainder of the weekend to explore. Things could not have been any better. We spent the afternoon wandering through Madrid's narrow streets and public plazas, large and small. We ate a late dinner at the hotel's rooftop restaurant, and an even later breakfast on Sunday with the remainder of the day strolling through the city's parks and marveling at the architecture, relatively untouched by the ravages of the wars that destroyed so much of Europe's history. Dinner was a selection of tapas consumed at a streetside café, accompanied by an excellent bottle of a Rioja red from Spain's north. That night, as we were going to bed, Jenna said, "You know, John, we've only been here a couple of days, but being with you and having all the other distractions of both of our lives so far away, it makes me realize how much I love you." Almost at that moment, I considered asking her to marry me, but thought better of it, still planning on the Prado.

On Monday, Tuesday and part of Wednesday, we shopped for inventory at the fair. Getting the paintings and other works of art delivered to the gallery was no problem. Such events always feature shipping services that specialize in such. Once a piece has been purchased, the shipper is notified, the artwork crated or packed, and then sent by the most convenient route, usually via air. With Jenna's advice, which turned out to be quite insightful, I had purchased fifteen paintings on canvas, two dozen-plus serigraphs, and six small ceramic pieces that we thought would sell well in the Savannah market. The weather remained kind, allowing us to stroll about in the late afternoon and evening, dining late per Spanish custom at restaurants recommended by the hotel's concierge. On Thursday we took a daytrip by train to Toledo, and on Friday, a private guided tour to Segovia to marvel at the two-thousand-year-old Roman aqueduct. Our flight back to the States was scheduled to depart shortly after noon on Sunday. I planned to offer the ring to Jenna on Saturday.

As this could be one of the most important decisions of my life, I had made my plans carefully. In order to control the number of visitors at any one time, tickets to the Museo del Prado are sold by time of entry. To avoid the weekend crowds as much as possible I purchased two tickets online for the opening time of 10:00 a.m. on Saturday morning. Studying the museum's floor plan, I thought we'd spend a short while rambling about as I subtly guided Jenna toward room 56A, where *The Garden of Earthly Delights* adorned one wall. I expected that she would marvel at the painting, its beauty, and its graphic depiction of joy and happiness and love. At that point I planned to produce the ring and ask her to marry me. After that, we would have a full day and night to celebrate before departing for home. I had planned it carefully. Nothing could go wrong.

I carried the ring in its red leather pouch in my pants pocket from Savannah to Madrid, never taking it out with the constant assurance that it would not set off a metal detector. At the hotel, I'd secreted it behind the zip-out lining of my suitcase. On Saturday morning, before breakfast, I took it out of its hiding place and slipped it in my pocket while Jenna was in the bathroom. She'd told me the night before that this had been one of the most wonderful weeks of her life, but clearly had no idea of my plans. Rather than walk this time, we took a taxi to the museum and were among the first to enter as the doors opened for the day. I kept nervously reaching into my pocket to be sure the pouch was still there. After about half an hour of marveling at the art works, we arrived at room 56A. It was empty except for an elderly couple and their English-speaking guide who was finishing up his explanation of the painting.

Jenna stared at the colorful canvas, her eyes wide and an uncertain look on her face. I noted that she took several deep breaths. "It's beautiful, isn't it?" I asked.

She continued to stare, not responding at first, then replied, "It's *The Garden of Earthly Delights*," followed by another deep breath.

"Yes," I said, thinking she remembered it from her art history courses in college. "But it's more than that. It's about love and joy and bliss, and all the pleasures life can bring." I fingered the pouch in my pocket, preparing to present her with the ring. "Think of the name, 'earthly delights,' of the possibilities of happiness our world can offer, if we just try…."

Jenna didn't respond, her gaze fixed on the painting. "John," she said, her voice grim, " I know the painting. We studied it in school. It's so much more than that. There's the Garden of Eden there," she said, pointing to the left panel. "The god-figure is presenting Eve to Adam, and all is well with the beautiful world. And then, there," she continued, pointing to the larger center panel, "are the peoples of the earth, descendants of Adam and Eve, blissfully enjoying all the pleasures that life can offer." Jenna paused, swallowed and took another deep breath. "And then, there on the right, is the artist's vision of Hell, with torture and pain. That's what happened to us, John. Our lives were going well, or so we thought, and then we descended into Hell." She looked like she was about to cry. I took my hand out of my pocket.

I didn't know how to respond. I didn't know what to say. I took Jenna gently by her elbow and led her to the next room, now empty of museum visitors. We sat down on an upholstered bench. "I'm sorry," I said. "I didn't realize you were familiar with the painting. And I didn't know it would upset you."

Jenna was dabbing at her eyes with a tissue she'd taken from her pocket. "It's not your fault. You had no way of knowing—remember, you didn't even know I'd taken a few art courses in school. There's more to it than that."

"How so?"

"A friend, a close friend in fact. Mindy. She was an art major."

"You've never mentioned her."

"No, I guess not," Jenna replied still dabbing at her eyes. "That was one of her favorite paintings. She said it described life exactly. I remember laughing when she said that, and told her how silly it was. I told her I planned to marry, to raise a family, to be successful at something in life. And then…." Jenna's voice trailed off.

"Where is Mindy now?" I asked.

"They never found her body," Jenna replied, this time sobbing as the tears streamed down her cheeks.

CHAPTER 4

My glorious plan to ask Jenna to marry me had been a complete disaster. After a few minutes of sitting silently on the bench, she took my hand and said, "John, I'm so sorry. I…, I shouldn't have reacted like that. This has been a delightful week, and up until a few moments ago, this had been a wonderful day, but…." Her voice trailed off, seemingly for a loss of words. I continued to hold her hand, waiting for her to say more. She dabbed at her eyes again then said, "The problem is all mine, and I don't need to take it out on you—or spoil our trip. But just seeing that painting brought up memories that I've tried to forget, memories about a very bad time in my life." She raised her head and turned to look directly into my eyes. "Can you forgive me? Please?"

"Of course," I said. "I care about you. I love you."

Jenna put her arms around me and buried her head on my chest. "And I love you." She hesitated again, then, "I promise I'll explain all this when the time is right. But for now, let's try to enjoy ourselves before we have to go home." She stood up, grabbed my hand and led me gently toward the museum's exit.

We spent most of the rest of the day lazily walking about the huge Retiro park, sharing tapas for lunch at a small lakeside café before returning to the hotel for a nap before dinner. I had made reservations at the Four Season's premiere restaurant for what was supposed to have been a private celebration before we returned home and announced our engagement to the world. There were so very many things I wanted to say to Jenna. Thoughts and feelings and plans and hopes that I wanted to share with her. Instead, we shared a bottle of pricy Catalonian cava that the sommelier insisted was on a par with the finest French champagne. After the second glass, Jenna apologized once again for the scene at the museum. I assured her all was well, even though I wasn't totally certain. Once more, she promised to share the story with me sometime, but the memory of her cryptic comment about never finding Mindy's body hovered in the background.

The flight back to Atlanta, nearly ten hours this time due to strong headwinds, went smoothly. Jenna seemed to be back to her familiar self, saying several times how much she enjoyed the trip and how much she would miss being with me. After an uneventful drive home, we were back in Savannah by late afternoon. Jenna seemed reluctant to leave, but needed to get to Claxton to pick up her son and thank her parents for taking care of him in her absence. I trudged up the steps from the courtyard to my apartment, suddenly lonely. Despite the temptation, I had managed to avoid calling the gallery the entire time we were away, and now I suppressed the urge to call Jessica to see what had happened. A bit jet-lagged—it was just past midnight in Madrid—I decided to go to bed and deal with things the following morning.

Jenna called early Monday, still all bubbly about the trip. Her son had experienced no problems, and she was headed back to work. All was well at the gallery. Both Hattie and Jessica were there to open the shop, eager to hear about Madrid and the new inventory that was on the way. Like a video that had been put on pause, my life seemed to be resuming where I'd left off ten or so days earlier, with nothing really changed. As much as I was disappointed about the episode at the Prado, I still wanted to ask Jenna to marry me. But before that could happen, I realized I needed to have a better understanding about Mindy, and indeed many things in Jenna's past life that could become minefields on our future path together. After tossing it about in my head for several days, I resolved that if she did not voluntarily follow through with her promise to tell me what happened, I would gently insist on it, justifying my concern as a lover and a friend. If she refused to discuss this, and perhaps other things that she might be hiding, I would need to make some very difficult decisions about our relationship.

The next weeks flew by quickly, fulfilling the adage that every day away from a business generates at least two days of new work on returning. I spent many hours in my office, for the most part dealing with trivial issues that required my personal touch. Sales at the gallery had continued to thrive, with several regular customers eagerly awaiting the arrival of the shipment from Spain and the annual migration of summer visitors swelling the ranks of shoppers. I was seeing Jenna at least twice a week now. The subject of Mindy did not come up, and I deliberately avoided mention of anything that might force the issue. I was waiting—perhaps vainly—for Jenna to say something, to follow through with her promise. As events would happen, however, it was fate instead that would eventually thrust the matter back into the spotlight.

On the day after Jenna and I left for Spain, Daniel Wilson, a real estate agent specializing in commercial properties, was exploring a large tract of land just off Interstate-16 in the southern part of Bulloch County. For decades it had served as cropland, but the growth of the port of Savannah had spurred industrial development in the area. A large firm involved in the manufacture of lithium batteries was viewing this site, along with others, for a possible new plant. With plat in hand and wearing high-top boots to help avoid snakebite, Wilson was walking along a small hedgerow on the edge of a hayfield when the morning sun reflected from a shiny object near the base of a young chinaberry tree. Curious, he stopped and stepped carefully into the weedy springtime growth to see what it was. To his surprise, it was a thick metal necklace, no doubt made of some inexpensive material which allowed it to retain its luster, but otherwise worthless. He examined it and tossed it back on the earth, wondering how it ended up there "in the middle of nowhere" as he later told police. In doing so, he noticed another shiny object nearby, barely protruding from the ground. Bending over to pick it up, he realized that it was tangled about a whitish object, a stick of some sort. He nudged it with his boot, and in that moment realized the "stick" was in fact a bone. He reached in his pocket for his cell phone and began making calls.

Within two hours the hayfield was full of vehicles belonging to the Bulloch County Sheriff's Office and the Georgia State Patrol. Shortly thereafter a crime scene investigation team from the Coastal branch of the State Crime Laboratory arrived. It appeared that the hedgerow hid the burial site of a body, presumably a female based on the jewelry. The landowner was contacted and interviewed. He had no knowledge of any such burial but opined that since his field was near the expressway and not too distant from an exit, perhaps someone might have been attempting to conceal a crime. Over the next twenty-four hours the crime scene team photographed and carefully exhumed the remainder of the skeleton of which the protruding bone was part. Other than several pieces of nondescript jewelry, there was little else to help identify the person who was assumed to be a murder victim buried in a shallow grave. The adjacent soil was sifted for other physical evidence or clues. None of major significance were found. The bones of the skeleton were carefully placed in containers to be taken back to the lab for further analysis.

The discovery of a skeleton buried in a shallow grave in rural Bulloch County earned a brief one-column article in the *Statesboro Herald*, accompanied by a single photo of the crime lab van, and an even shorter one-paragraph mention in the *Savannah Morning News*. The body appeared to have been buried years earlier. The crime, assuming it was such, was ancient history. Both articles mentioned that efforts would be made to identify the nameless deceased, now referred to as "the victim."

Weeks passed. In the United States, nearly half of all homicides are never solved. The state of Georgia has a slightly better track record, but in at least a third of the cases, the killer is never identified. The crime lab was able to determine that the victim was female, probably in her early to mid-twenties. She appeared to have had excellent dental care as a child, hinting she may have come from at least a middle-class background. No buttons or similar items were found in the soil around the skeleton, raising the possibility that she was naked when she was buried. The jewelry—the necklace, silver stud earrings, three bracelets, and a ring, was unremarkable. The lab was able to extract some assayable DNA from two molars. Because of the nature of the crime and a backlog in testing inhouse at the state laboratory, samples were submitted to two separate outside laboratories for analysis, both of which confirmed the same DNA profile. In the absence of any other identifiable findings, the results were submitted for comparison with the CODIS database, an FBI-maintained national repository of DNA profiles contributed by federal, state, and local participating forensic laboratories. No match was identified. Having reached a practical dead end, the investigation came to a standstill, another cold case. The profile of the unknown victim's DNA remained in the database.

CHAPTER 5

The artworks we purchased in Spain arrived with surprising speed, the graphic art within two weeks of our return to Savannah and the sculptures, which were bulky and required special handling, about three weeks later. My angst over Jenna's reaction to the painting had faded with time. As often as I was seeing her now, she seemed to have returned to her former self, the person I'd come to adore. And my perception of the whole episode had changed. Perhaps I should have thought of the painting as the equivalent of a giant Rorschach inkblot. I studied the canvas and saw one thing; Jenna viewed it and saw another. We had both experienced dark days during the course of our lives, things we were ashamed of and deeply regretted. In Bosch's work I saw a hopeful future. Yet, for Jenna, the same images raised specters from her past. No matter, really; the validity of the whole process was pretty uncertain anyway. For the moment, I decided to wait on discussing marriage with her. I made a quick trip to the bank and put the ring and its red leather pouch back in the safe deposit locker, though leaving it on top in the rosewood box so I could find it easily next time, if there was to be a next time.

Meanwhile, across town in Savannah's suburbs, some ten miles to the west of my gallery on Liberty Street, a conference committee at the branch offices of the State Crime Laboratory made the decision to submit the DNA profile of the anonymous Bulloch County victim to one of several services that specialized in tracking down genetic relatives of unknown DNA profiles. Over the preceding decade, the popularity of so-called "test-tube genealogy" had spawned a number of companies offering DNA analysis to the paying public, often solving genetic mysteries, revealing the geographic origin of one's ancestors, the recognition of genes potentially associated with the development of certain diseases, and, in some cases, the unfortunate revelation of true parentage. The information in their databases is private but with permission, or with a subpoena in criminal cases, investigators can obtain access. These services in turn gave birth to even more specialized firms whose focus is forensic genetic genealogy, especially in cases of murder, rape or anonymous human remains. In contrast to the highly technical task of defining a DNA profile, forensic genetics searches primarily for blood relatives of the individual whose specimen is being examined. In this case, the search would attempt to identify one or more persons with a genetic connection to the dead woman, thus creating a starting point for further investigation. The task is a tedious one, often requiring months before discovering a useful link or reaching a dead end.

Perhaps needless to say, neither Jenna nor I were aware of the discovery of the presumed murder victim in Bulloch County or of the search for her identity. May turned into June, and June into July. Having deferred my plans to start a new life together with Jenna, I was prepared to maintain the status quo, secretly hoping for a sign, an event, or an omen to point the way forward. I cared deeply about her, and was sure that she felt the same about me, but neither of us seemed to have the courage to move forward as one, or move on to the uncertain future of other lovers.

The infusion of new inventory brought a swell in sales, often to collectors or repeat customers, but also to new clients who had heard about the gallery. During the month of July, we featured the European pieces in conjunction with exhibits by local artists, rotating displays of the latter every week. By mid-month, Hattie proudly informed me that our sales volume had increased to the point that we had recouped the entire cost of the trip to Madrid, in addition to earning a healthy profit on top of that. I left the gallery early for a change, retreating to the air-conditioned coolness of my apartment to avoid the summer heat, and to think about the future.

Months earlier, before our trip to Madrid, Jenna had referred to the apartment as my "safe space," a place where I could hide from the woes of the world. She had asked me, "Isn't it time to be yourself?" She was right, and while life would certainly continue to have its ups and downs, I couldn't hide forever. So, I made the decision to do two things. I would move across the courtyard to my grandparents' big house, and I would once again plan to ask Jenna to marry me, hoping to avoid a repeat of the debacle in the Prado. This time I would try for something romantic but low-key, perhaps a candlelit dinner and a bottle of Dom Perignon to set the stage. Savannah has a number of restaurants with private dining rooms. Or perhaps I could entertain her with a catered dinner in the grand dining room of the new house. As long as I had a plan, I could work out the details later. My mind made up once again, I ate a light supper and went to bed early.

I was out of bed, showered and dressed by six-thirty the next morning, eager to follow through with my planning. The gallery did not open until ten, although Jessica usually arrived about half an hour earlier. I wanted to walk through my new home. I knew it well of course; I had spent many months there while growing up, often foisted upon my grandparents while my bipolar mother pursued her latest romantic entanglement. The high-ceilinged rooms with their ornate furniture and gilt-edged mirrors, the oriental carpets and heavy drapes were vestiges of another time, another generation. For me they held many memories, of my mother's drug and alcohol-fueled rages, of my grandparents' unconditional love, of my desire to lead a normal life, whatever that meant. All that was in the past now. Other than my two children, whom my ex-wife refused to let me see, I was the only surviving member of my family. I had a chance now to make a new start, hopefully with Jenna by my side. This would be the place.

The house was four stories in height, constructed in the 1870s by a wealthy merchant on the site of an earlier home that had been damaged by fire. The art gallery was located on the ground floor, the part of the home that originally housed the servants' quarters. The next level, accessed by a formal set of double steps rising from the sidewalk, held the living and dining rooms, parlor, library, kitchen and related public spaces. The third and fourth levels were each divided into three generous bedrooms opening into a common area used as a sort of informal family room. The upper levels had large rear porches, with steps leading down from one to the other and then to the courtyard separating the main structure from my apartment above the old carriage house, which itself faced a wide alleyway in the rear. The old house was too big, of course, but I thought I could be happy living there. What could I do with six bedrooms? But then there was the possibility of another child with Jenna, if things worked out. Or a reconciliation with my two children whom I had not seen since going to prison. The future was as uncertain as my past life had been unpredictable. I yearned for stability, for predictability, and perhaps even for the reassuring boredom of an ordinary existence.

I was descending the steps from the second level just as Jessica drove into the courtyard and parked her car near the gallery's rear entrance. "Oh! You frightened me," she said, a pleased look on her face. "Were you checking out the big house? Maybe thinking about moving in? I'm sure you don't want or need my opinion, but I'll give it anyway. I think it would be a great idea. You're doing so well. Time to move up in the world." Without giving me a chance to respond, she unlocked the door and disappeared into the gallery. I glanced at my watch. It was 9:39 a.m.

Just at that moment my cell phone rang. Jenna's name and photo appeared on the screen. Smiling, I touched the green phone icon and said, "Good morning! This is a surprise. Are you at work?" At first I heard nothing, then what sounded like sobbing at the other end of the line. "Jenna? Is that you? Are you okay? Talk to me, please."

There was a pause, the sound of rapid breathing, then, "Oh, John, oh, John…."

"What? Please tell me what happened—what's going on?"

"I just got a call. They found Mindy's body."

CHAPTER 6

Between sobs, Jenna explained that she had just received a call from Mindy's mother, a Mrs. Davis, from Vidalia, Georgia. Someone from the Bulloch County Sheriff's Office had called her to say they had discovered what were thought to be her daughter's remains. Jenna didn't know any more than that, but planned to drive to Mindy's mother's house after she arranged for someone to look after her son. She said she was too upset to talk now, but promised to call me later when she knew the details.

I wasn't sure what I should do. My first reaction was the urge to be with Jenna, to comfort her, to help see her through this tragedy. But then, she had not yet explained her relationship to Mindy, and she had to know that I gladly would have gone with her if she simply asked. I decided it would be best for me to wait for her call.

As I would learn later, the State Crime Laboratory had contracted with an Atlanta-based forensic genealogy company named MatchDNA to see if the firm could find a genetic match for the autosomal DNA profile extracted from the skeleton found in Bulloch County. The company had access to a number of public and private DNA databases, and equally importantly, employed a team of individuals skilled at searching missing person reports, unsolved crime databases, newspaper articles and other sources for potential clues to the identity of the young woman. Focusing first on the southeastern United States, one group of investigators compiled a list of missing females of the estimated age of the victim. Meanwhile, a second group compared her DNA to genetic records found in multiple databases, essentially all collected from individuals curious to learn their heritage or family relationships. Kinships such as cousins, siblings, and parents are readily identified, as are indications of ethnicity and familial origins of prior generations. A potential clue was quickly discovered.

Some ten years earlier, a young man named Daniel Peter Davis, Jr. gave his parents a Christmas gift of genetic testing by a company named Family Tree DNA, promising to trace the migration patterns of male ancestors for up to five generations in the past. Peter had tested himself first and received a result that his lineage was primarily from the British Isles, more specifically from Wales. His father often claimed a Welsh heritage; Peter thought it would please him to have this confirmed. The genetic profiles of the three Davises were entered into the company's database. Permission was granted to allow the company to check for other genetic matches in hopes of finding unknown relatives. In such cases, the Davises would be contacted. Peter's father, Dr. Daniel Peter Davis, Sr., died unexpectedly of a stroke some five months later, leaving his widow and two children, Peter, Jr., and a daughter named Mary Nelle.

MatchDNA investigators honed in on the match between the unknown DNA and that of the Davis family. It appeared genetically certain that the deceased was the daughter of the two parents, and that the younger man, Peter, Jr., was her brother. With a potential name in hand, the other investigative group found a missing person report for a twenty-seven year old female named Mary Nelle Davis, who was thought to likely be the unidentified victim. The information and supporting data were turned over to the Crime Lab and immediately passed on to the appropriate agents of the Georgia Bureau of Investigation.

The remainder of the day passed slowly. Something terrible had happened. Something that involved someone I believed I loved, which meant that it involved me as well. I found myself nervously looking at my phone every few minutes to see if I had somehow missed a text or not heard a phone call. It was just after three in the afternoon before Jenna called. She sounded calmer this time, but I read emotion in her voice. "I'm headed back to my apartment in Claxton. Robert will be staying with my parents for at least tonight," she said, referring to her son. There was a long pause, leading me to think I had lost the connection, then, "John, is there any way you can come over here for the night? I don't want to be alone." Another pause. "And we have to talk." I readily agreed, letting Jessica know that Jenna had an unspecified emergency and that I needed to be with her.

"I'll plan on being back in the morning."

"I'm so sorry." Jessica said. "I hope she's not ill," thinking I'd volunteer a more specific reason for leaving so suddenly. "No, her close friend died," I explained, not bothering to mention it apparently happened years earlier. The tour of my grandparents' house forgotten, I hurried over to my apartment, stuffed a quick change of clothes in an overnight bag and headed toward Claxton.

I arrived at Jenna's apartment about four-thirty. She lived on the second floor of a modest four-unit building, one of very few in the small community of about 2,500 inhabitants. The grass in the yard was shaggy; the window trim needed a fresh coat of paint. I knocked on the door, then tried the knob. It was unlocked. The blinds were drawn, darkening the living room. A noisy air conditioner pumped in cool air to offset the summer heat. I called Jenna's name, realizing almost immediately that she appeared to be napping in an oversized recliner. "Oh," she said, evidently surprised. "I'm sorry—I must have drifted off. It's been a bad day, John." She rose and hugged me. "I'm glad you're here. I need you to help me through this." I asked her if I could get her anything—food perhaps, as I suspected she hadn't eaten. She said she wasn't hungry. "Let me start at the beginning—when I was in college—and tell you about things...." She swallowed, looked down, then back at me. "...and about Mindy and the rest of my life. I think you need to know, to understand who I am, and who I was and who I've become."

A cold shiver flowed over me. "Okay," I said, fearful of what she was about to say.

Jenna switched on a table lamp next to a large comfortable sofa, indicating I should sit at one end. She sat at the other and turned to face me, drawing her legs up with her arms around them. "It seems like several lifetimes ago, maybe when I was fifteen or sixteen, I realized that one day I would be what they called an adult, and at the same time realized I had no idea what I wanted to do with my life. No one in my family had ever attended college. My father dropped out in the tenth grade to work on the family farm, and my mother barely managed to make it through her high school graduation. They married the following week, and I was born shortly after my mother's twentieth birthday. They both worked at ordinary jobs—my dad is pretty smart and before he was thirty he'd become a supervisor at the local poultry plant. We weren't poor, but we didn't have a lot. They're content with their place in life. I think they sort of assumed I would do the same—finish high school, get married, have kids and all that. But I made good grades, in fact I almost always was the top scorer on the achievement tests they make you take. My teachers pushed me to go to college, but my parents were quick to tell me we couldn't afford it. So, with the help of my high school guidance counselor, I applied for a bunch of scholarships, and to everyone's surprise I was granted a full ride at Georgia Southern. It paid for everything, tuition, room and board, books, and even gave me a little bit of spending money." I sat silently, listening. I had met her parents. They seemed to be well-adjusted, salt of the earth folk, happy to be living in a rural Georgia town. At the same time, I could understand why Jenna wanted more.

Jenna continued. "College was easy, all considered. I didn't try to pledge a sorority—I didn't have the money—but I had plenty of friends. I won't say Statesboro is exactly the big city, but for someone raised in Claxton, it was a change. I saw and experienced and tried all sorts of new things—I guess we all do that when we move away from home—but I kept up my GPA thinking maybe I wanted to go to graduate school. I dated a bunch of guys, but in my junior year met Carl. He was an SAE (ΣAE), majoring in English Lit and planning to go to law school. We ended up getting married the summer after we graduated, just because it seemed that was what we were supposed to do. Looking back on things, I'm not sure I was ever really in love with him. And then things happened. Carl got turned down by every law school he applied to. He took a job as a real estate agent. And I got pregnant. I like to think it was an accident, because I hadn't planned on it, and we weren't ready. But it worked out. Robert was born just before I turned twenty-four.

"And I need to tell you about Mindy. She was from Vidalia—and she was my very best friend." Jenna hesitated, seemingly pained at even mentioning her name. "I guess I should say that in so many ways she was the complete opposite of me. Her parents were well-to-do. Her father was a doctor; he died suddenly when we were in college. I was the girl who always tried to do the right thing, but Mindy was a free spirit, a wild child, very smart but always willing to try something new. She was an art major, and in fact went on to get her master's degree in art history after we graduated. She was the one that introduced me to art, and that's why I took several electives in that when I was a junior and senior." As she spoke, Jenna seemed to choke up as a tear streaked down her cheek. She reached over to grab a tissue from a box on the end table and continued, "And that painting, *The Garden of Earthly Delights*, was her favorite. She had a large copy of it hanging on the wall of her apartment and was always talking about it, referring to it, explaining her interpretation of the symbolism. 'That's the life I want,' she'd say. 'I want to find my own garden of earthly delights before I'm too old to enjoy it.'"

CHAPTER 7

"I'd like to hear more about Mindy," I said.

"Yes, I'm getting to that. Mindy was probably the closest friend I've ever had. Since I got the call yesterday from her mother saying they'd discovered her body, I've been thinking about it constantly. I realized it's hard to know about me without knowing about Mindy, and I don't...." Jenna paused, "...I guess I almost don't know where to start. But let me tell you a story that maybe describes her and how her brain worked.

"Mindy's real name was Mary Nelle Davis. It's an old person's name—Mary Nelle—in fact she was named for her grandmother, her father's mother. That was not at all who she was or thought she wanted to be. So, we were talking late one night, and I asked her how she got her nickname. She told me that when she was in the seventh or eighth grade, someone—the same grandmother, I think—gave her a monogrammed sweater. She hated it for some reason, but her mother insisted she wear it to school, and of course the other kids asked about the 'MND' letters. She told me she just explained to them that was the other way of spelling her real name, which was 'Mindy.' That doesn't make sense of course, but these were twelve or fourteen year old kids, and thereafter everyone who knew her called her 'Mindy.' She was like that, artsy, thinking-outside-the-box, always wanting to try something new, to push the limits.

"We met on the first day of registration at college. Neither one of us knew anybody, and were both were sorta insecure about starting out on our own in a new place. We ended up standing next to each other in one of those long lines, so we talked and realized we'd each made our first friend there. Mindy was not into sororities—she could have afforded joining—but said she didn't like having to do what other people wanted her to do, so she didn't go out for rush. I guess in most ways we were opposites, me being the first member of my family to go to college and relying on a scholarship to pay for it, and her from a family where everyone was well educated and had plenty of money. For whatever reason, though, we seemed to hit it off and started hanging out together.

"That's how it started. We saw a lot of each other over the next four years. I visited her home in Vidalia and she came to mine in Claxton. We even dated some of the same guys—not at the same time, of course. The art classes I took were ones Mindy recommended, and that's where I first saw the painting—I'll get to that part of the story in a minute. Anyway, I started dating Carl and things just kind of worked out and we went exclusive. But Mindy had lots of interests and that includes men. She'd go out with someone for a few months and then dump him for some other guy. That was just her thing. It wasn't that there was anything wrong with whoever she was dating, it was more that she liked variety and something new. And I guess that was another way we were different. I just sort of settled in with Carl, and did what I thought you were supposed to do—find someone you could live with and marry him. So, I did." Jenna looked down as if the admission was painful. "About the only good thing that came of that was Robert, my son. And while I was getting married and supposedly setting out on this long journey with my husband, Mindy decided to go on and get her master's in art history."

"Where did the painting, *The Garden of Earthly Delights*, come in?" I asked, thinking the story was wandering off to other things.

"I'm getting to that," Jenna said, seeming slightly annoyed that I had interrupted her. "So, while I was planning my wedding to Carl, Mindy was headed back to school. We were both still going to be living in Statesboro near the college for the next year at least, so we decided to move in together. That worked fine. Mindy still dated around, but not nearly as much, and I was engaged and had gotten a job, so my life calmed down, too. She absolutely loved school, and would often spend an hour or more explaining how the mind of an artist works, or the hidden meaning of some painting or another, or the 'power of symbolism' as she called it. And there was one professor—Dr. Martinez—who she thought was just the greatest. I remember she said he was an 'adjunct' professor, a word I had never heard. I thought maybe that meant he was an expert or had a specialist degree in something, but she explained that it meant he was not on the regular faculty, but contracted by the college to teach a certain course on Art of the Renaissance. I don't know much more than that, but he was the one who turned her on to the Bosch painting. Mindy had the money, so she ordered a huge copy of the *Earthly Delights* painting that took up most of one of the walls of our living room. And every now and then we'd sit there and drink a glass of wine and she would explain—or attempt to explain—the meaning behind whatever the naked figures cavorting across the canvas were doing. She kept saying that whether we recognized it or not, the course of our lives was there for us to see—the only thing being that we didn't know—or couldn't know—which of the figures foretold our future.

"So, we went on like that for a good while," Jenna continued. "I had a small wedding—my parents couldn't afford to do much to help, so Carl and I paid for most of it. Mindy was my maid of honor, and of course we drifted apart after I moved in with Carl in Savannah. I'll leave out all that happened, but my marriage turned out to be pure hell—kinda like in the painting, I guess. Carl started drinking, I got pregnant and had to quit my job once the baby was born. It's a long story, but in the end we separated and I moved back home to Claxton with my parents and Carl filed for divorce. He was supposed to pay child support, but stopped after a few months. I know he was fired from his real estate job and I'm not sure what he did after that. I guess I could have turned him in and let the child support enforcers make his life miserable, but instead I just decided to do the best I could, just Robert and me. And that's when I made the mistake of linking back up with Mindy."

Jenna now seemed nervous, hesitant, uncomfortable at where her story appeared to be heading. She sat up, saying, "I'm going to get a bottle of water out of the 'fridge. Do you want anything, John?" I told her I was fine, and momentarily she settled back on her end of the sofa. After taking a couple of sips, she continued. "I hadn't seen Mindy in a good while, six months at least. We had talked, of course, but only occasionally and then never in detail. She had finished up her master's, and I assumed she would be teaching somewhere, or working in an art gallery or museum. She wasn't. She said she had a new job, but didn't want to talk much about it over the phone. And the good part, she said, was that she worked nights, so she could sleep late every morning. I couldn't decide if she was making a joke or what, but I didn't say anything. Mindy knew about the divorce of course, but didn't know how bad my situation was with Carl refusing to offer any support for our son and so on. We talked a bit more, and then she suggested that I come visit her at work. They might have something for me to do there. She said the pay was not great, but the tips more than made up for it. Some weeks she took home more than a thousand dollars, and it was all cash. She had me at that. I said I'd love to visit. She told me she was working at a restaurant off I-95 just south of Savannah, and gave me the address."

Jenna shifted again, clearly uneasy. I knew some of her history, but had not heard this before and wasn't sure where the story was leading. "Are you okay?" I asked. "You don't have to tell me anything you don't want to. What's in the past—for both of us—can stay there."

"I need to finish what I started to say," she said, and continued. "I looked up the address online so I had no trouble finding it. It was a Friday, and Mindy had suggested that I come by that night about nine o'clock. That suited me fine, as I could drop my son off at my parents around eight, then drive to Savannah to see where Mindy worked. It turned out the 'restaurant' was a 'gentleman's club.' I guess it did serve food, but more importantly it had a bar and a dance stage. I walked in just in time to see Mindy on up there, hanging on a pole, and essentially naked. A gaggle of rough-looking men were sitting at the base of the stage, catcalling at her and waving cash, which she'd grab and stuff under a garter on her thigh. Besides being mostly naked, the second thing I noticed was that she'd lost weight, a lot of it. She saw me from the stage, quickly finished up her routine and disappeared into a door at the back of the stage. Two minutes later she came rushing out of a side door, now wrapped up in a robe, and hugged my neck. I remember exactly what she said: 'I am so glad you're here, Jenna! You'd be just perfect!' She reached into the pocket of her robe and pulled out a handful of ten and twenty dollar bills. She'd made more in one dance than I often made in a day at my current job. And that was just the beginning."

CHAPTER 8

"Mindy was all keyed up, much more so than even her usual self. As I said, I hadn't seen her in a number of months. I knew she was glad to see me as her friend, but in a vague way things just seemed a little over the top. We chatted for a few minutes; I would have been uncomfortable sitting there wearing nothing but a G-string under a robe with a steady stream of men crowding in to tell me how good I looked, but she seemed to take it in stride, as if this was just another Friday night. And for her, maybe it was...."

I interrupted her. "Jenna, I know your history. I know you were working as a stripper. You told me—no, showed me—not all that long after we met. You don't have to tell me this. You don't have to explain...."

"I didn't tell you everything, John. I didn't explain about the drugs and...."

"I don't need to know. I care about you so very much. Not the you that you were when things were bad, but who you are now, the woman I love."

"You need to know. You need to know everything, and how it happened." She stopped, seemingly waiting for my reply.

I was torn. I was so fearful that she had something terrible to say, something that would bring an immediate end to our relationship. But in that moment I decided if there were dark secrets, it would be better to know them now than later when circumstances might be different. I nodded and quietly said, "Okay."

"Anyway, I stayed there at the club for a couple of hours. The place was full of friendly people, and I let a guy buy me a glass of wine. Thinking back on it now, it was the first time I'd been out since the divorce, and I realized that I enjoyed it—the music, the conversation, just being free for even a short while, away from living with my parents and taking care of Robert. Mindy was back and forth—she did one more dance and then came and sat with me at a table. That attracted several good-looking guys who kinda began to hit on me, something else that hadn't happened in a long, long time. Mindy suggested that she might be able to get me a job as a waitress on the week-ends. They were always short of help. And she reminded me about the tips. I told her I would think about it. I hated my day job and was pretty miserable at home, so by the time I got back to my parents', I'd decided to try it.

"I started the next weekend. I met with the manager and agreed to work on Friday and Saturday nights from seven until closing and cleanup, which usually meant I could leave an hour or two past midnight. Sometimes I'd drive home, but mostly I stayed at Mindy's place—a lot of times by myself if she had a date. Being a waitress was something new for me, and it didn't take too long to realize this was not a family restaurant. Most of the customers were men, and most of them were there to drink and see the girls on stage. The head waitress told me how to get bigger tips, be super-friendly, wear a push-up bra and act sexy. I was kind of insulted by that at first. I didn't say anything but it didn't take too long to realize she was right.

"The other thing was my weight. I wasn't fat, but I hadn't really lost all the weight I gained with my pregnancy. Between work and taking care of Robert, I didn't have much time for exercise. I tried going to a gym, but found out I was too busy even for that. And the gym membership was expensive, too, so I gave up and just bought clothes a size or two larger. We were sitting around at Mindy's one Friday night after work and I told her that I thought I was too fat. She said she had some pills that someone had given her—I thought she meant a doctor but I found out later that was wrong. They really helped her lose weight, and probably helped with the tips, too. She said she'd give me a few, but wanted me to be sure I took them in the morning because one other thing they did was decrease your need for sleep. And that's how I got started on meth."

Jenna seemed to be waiting on my reaction. I said nothing. She had told me not long after we met that she had a problem with methamphetamine at one time in the past, but was no longer abusing. I didn't know where all this was going. I hadn't asked, but it was my understanding that the meth had some connection with her run-in with the law. Before now I had never asked for details; she had never volunteered them. After a moment of silence I asked, "Why are you telling me all this?"

"Because in the last few months you have told me dozens of times that you love me. I don't know what the future will hold for either one of us, but I don't want there to be any surprises, either for you or for me. Is that reason enough?"

"If it's what you feel is best, then go ahead...."

She took a deep breath and exhaled, then continued, "So, at first I took one pill once a day in the morning. And to be honest, it was great. I believe I was kinda depressed, but that seemed to go away on the first day. It was like one of those days when you've had a really good night's sleep and then wake up and have a huge cup of coffee and feel like you could conquer the world. I was—I thought—smarter, quicker and more clever than I'd ever been. At work they commented that I must be enjoying my job. But then later in the day, the high would wear off, and I'd feel really tired. So, every now and then I would take a second pill, especially on Friday and Saturday when I was working at the club. And as I lost a few pounds and gained more confidence, my tips got bigger. I thought the pills were magic. The guys kept hitting on me, telling me how good I looked, trying to get me to go out with them. I was feeling better about myself than I had in years. And then I made another stupid mistake, probably the biggest mistake of my life thus far.

"Between my day job and waitressing on the weekends, I was doing pretty good, I thought. But money was still tight, and by then I had started buying the weight loss pills that Mindy had first given me. I didn't know exactly what was in them, and if someone had told me it was meth, that probably wouldn't have stopped me from using them. I was taking more than I could bum off Mindy and I was running short every week. I said something to her about needing to make more, and she said she thought I could do real well dancing at the club. Looking back on things, the problem wasn't how much money I was making, it was how much I was spending, with a big chunk of that going to pills. And again, I took Mindy's advice and tried out—I started using the stage name of 'Candi'. And the money started flowing in. I'd make several hundred extra dollars a week. The guys seemed to love me and always wanted to buy me a drink, or offer to help me out if I needed a little extra money, thinking maybe they could get me to go out with them.

"You know, looking back on all this, I can't believe how naïve and stupid I was. I can't make any excuses. I should have seen the direction my life was taking. Mindy was my friend, and in many ways I both idolized and was jealous of her. But I was headed down the same rabbit hole and if I had thought about it, I would have realized that nothing good was going to come of it. Maybe I should blame the pills; after a while there was no doubt that I needed them, that I was hooked on them. Oh, I heard people say the stuff is even better if you smoke it, but I said to myself that's drug abuse for real addicts. I'm just taking a few pills to make my life better. I was such a fool." Jenna grabbed at a tissue and wiped the tears from her cheeks once again. I sat at the other end of the sofa, silent and expressionless.

"Tell me about your troubles with the law," I asked, a gentle rephrasing of "Did you get arrested?"

"But there's more. I haven't finished telling you about Mindy, and all that went on."

"I know, but I think I've heard enough to understand what happened."

A look of relief seemed to appear on Jenna's face. "Okay, I'll skip ahead several months. I was working at the club on weekends and at my day job during the week. There was no doubt I was hooked on the pills and kept lying to myself about being able to quit any time I wanted to. I had lost about twenty or twenty-five pounds, and was getting kinda skinny. My parents were concerned, thinking my 'restaurant' job might be hurting my health. I told them I was trying to slim down just in case I met a guy I wanted to go out with. They seemed fairly satisfied with that, at least until the night when they got the call from the Bryan County sheriff's deputy."

CHAPTER 9

"It was a Saturday night, one of the nights I usually spent with Mindy," Jenna began. "A lot of the time—most of the time, really—we'd have dates or go out for a while after work, no matter how late it was, and then sleep in on Sunday morning. But this night Mindy said she had a date with a 'special friend,' and it might be better if she had the apartment to herself—and him, or them, or whoever. Anyway, that was okay with me, because I'd been really busy at work and needed to get home to spend some time with Robert. So we finished up a bit early, maybe a little before one, and with all the customers gone had a quick couple of glasses of wine at the bar before heading home. As far as I know, Mindy went to her apartment to meet her date, and I got on the road back to Claxton. And the other thing was that the guy I was getting my pills from had come by the club late and dropped off a full bottle, enough to last me more than a month. He knew Saturday night was great for tips and I'd have some cash.

"I was headed west on US 280 between Pembroke and Claxton. The weather was good and the radio on, and of course I'd drank some wine just before leaving. I frankly don't remember what happened, but I must have started to doze off, because I sort of came to my senses and realized that I was drifting off the side of the highway. I tried jerking the car back on to the road, but by then I was on the right shoulder and ended up down on the grassy right-of-way maybe thirty feet or more from the edge of the pavement. My heart was pounding and I slammed on the brakes and came to a stop. I hadn't hit anything, and it looked like I could just pull back up on the road and be on my way. But when I tried the slope was too steep and I kept slipping back down. About that time, I saw some headlights coming up in the distance, and thought maybe I might get some help, especially when they began to slow and started to pull off the road. Then the blue lights came flashing on—it was a Bryan County sheriff's deputy.

"Ten minutes later he had me handcuffed and sitting in the back of the patrol car while he called for backup. I won't go into all the details, but I blew a 0.064 on the breathalyzer, and they found the bottle of pills I'd just gotten. They took me back to Pembroke, stuck me in a holding cell and initially charged me with DUI and Possession with Intent to Distribute for the pills. They said they'd give me one phone call, so I tried to reach Mindy. She didn't answer her cell. I told the jailer, who was a female deputy, that I needed to call my parents to check on my son and let them know where I was, but she snarled something about being 'out drinking and doping and not taking care of your kid' and said I could talk to the deputy on the next shift, which started at 6:00 a.m. Anyway, I eventually reached my parents and told them what happened. They got the magistrate judge to allow a $5,000 property bond, and I finally got home late Sunday afternoon."

For reasons I did not understand at the moment, Jenna now appeared calm and rather matter-of-fact as she recounted the details of her arrest. It seemed it all had been bottled up inside of her, that she wanted to tell me about it, but had been afraid to before. It was as if I were seeing her naked for the first time, observing her scars and imperfections and not reacting with shock or disgust. We have both been there, I thought, but merely said, "I'm glad you are sharing this with me. You had a rough time, I know…." For the first time since I'd arrived, I saw a quick smile form and disappear from her face.

"I could go into all the details of the months that followed," Jenna continued, "but it's easier if I just give you the highlights. A few weeks after the arrest, a Bryan County grand jury indicted me for the DUI and possession charges and scheduled a court date for about three months later. I kept my day job, but common sense and my parents both kept me from returning to the club. Mindy said she was so sorry about everything, and even came to visit me several times, but again we drifted apart. I guess I would have qualified for a public defender, but my father hired an attorney he knew from Pembroke. We all met and decided the quickest and best thing for me to do was try to get into a first-offender diversion program. This meant I'd have to plead guilty to all charges and agree to complete an intensive drug treatment program that included attending aftercare meetings for eighteen months. That's where I first met you." Jenna flashed a real smile this time, then continued. "If I did everything they asked, my record would be expunged and I could get on with my life. That happened, and now I'm totally legal. No more felonies."

"What about Mindy?" I asked.

"Like I said, we sort of lost touch. One of the requirements of the substance abuse treatment program was that I give up relationships with individuals and situations that had gotten me on drugs in the first place. I could not blame anyone but myself, but Mindy came in a close second in that regard. It was many months later that I heard she'd gone missing, and there was suspicion that she might have been murdered. Part of me—an emotional part—wanted to know all the details, but another more rational part said that whatever happened to her could have happened to me, so I didn't try at the time to find out. That doesn't mean she wasn't the closest friend I ever had. That connection and all the good memories were still there. I could try to suppress them, but couldn't erase them if I wanted to. I guess that's why I reacted that way to the painting in Madrid."

"Okay, then. I understand a lot of things now. I want to ask one more question. Not long after we first met, you wanted me to meet you at a club—not the one you and Mindy were working at, but another one out near the port area. You were still on stage, and still using the name of Candi."

Jenna smiled broadly this time, almost giving a small laugh. "Yes, I'd almost forgotten. The program I was in was a strict one, but importantly the people that designed it realized that no one can totally escape their previous life. There are toxic so-called 'friends' you can't totally avoid, workplaces with temptations and so on. We were encouraged to make a break with bad things from the past if possible, and if not, consider them as challenges to be overcome. And my problem was methamphetamine. Being an 'exotic dancer'—I prefer that term to 'stripper'—was probably the best and most profitable thing I could do to help support myself and my son. So, I took that challenge and managed to stay clean. I proved to myself I could do it. That's why I took you there, to make you understand more about me and my past. Things are so much better now. I have a great job, I'm proud of how my son is growing up, and I have you. I can't control the demons from my past. I will be the first to admit that. They are still there; they torture me sometimes, but every day brings a new chance to do the right thing." She appeared calm now.

I stayed with her that night. I had planned to do so, but first needed the reassurance she wanted my company. Driving back to Savannah the next morning, I thought about Jenna and her long and often detailed description of what had to be the darkest days of her life. She was a beautiful, talented, highly intelligent and well-educated person whose life had taken a number of wrong turns. Being as objective as I could, prior to the discovery of Mindy's body she seemed to be doing reasonably well psychologically. Under the calm façade, however, there were hidden currents of insecurity, shame, fear of rejection and others I had not recognized before. Her long soliloquy the day before had started with my simple request, "I'd like to hear more about Mindy." In some ways I felt like a priest who had just listened to a sinner confessing her sins, hoping her acknowledgment of them would lead to forgiveness, or if not that, tolerance. She said there was more, but I had heard enough. She saw and understood how she had erred. The person she had become, the person she was now was the one I knew and the one I had come to love. Blame was not appropriate, but if there was one person to be blamed, the one individual who helped drag Jenna into her morass, it was Mindy, her dearest friend and someone she no doubt loved. I worried what more the inevitable investigation of her death would yield, and wondered if Jenna had the same fears.

CHAPTER 10

After the initial shock of the discovery of Mindy's remains and the immediate reactions of those near to her wore off, I presumed the episode would gradually fade into memory. I was wrong. Certainly there were members of law enforcement who would continue to pursue the case so long as they had hope of finding her killer, and her family members would mourn for years, but for the rest of us with few personal connections it was simply another tragedy in a world in which such events were all too common. Jenna seemed sad, but within a few days appeared to be back to her usual self, no longer mentioning Mindy or making reference to their shared past. About three weeks later, however, she called, again upset. She had received an invitation to a memorial service followed by a phone call from Mindy's mother specifically requesting her presence. "It would mean so much to us," Mrs. Davis said. "You and my daughter were such close friends."

"I don't know, John," Jenna said. "A part of me says I've done all that I should or can. I'm not sure how I can add to that by dredging up everything again."

"I understand, but you should probably go. What's that old saying about funerals being for the living, not the dead? Mindy's father is deceased, and her mother has now lost one of her two children. I can only imagine the conversations that she's had to endure with those investigating her daughter's death—a girl with a bright future who ended up on drugs and working as a stripper in a bar...." I stopped, realizing that what I just said could have referred to Jenna as well. "I think it's what they call 'closure,' though I have no idea what that actually means."

She remained silent, not responding to my words. I quickly tried to soften the blow of my verbal gaffe. "How about I go with you, to provide some company and support if things get too intense?"

"Okay, I guess," Jenna said after a slight delay. "You're right. Mrs. Davis is hurting, and being there could be the one last thing I do for my friend's memory. I'll find out the details and let you know." She hung up without saying goodbye.

It was the next day before Jenna called back. To her surprise, the memorial service was to take place at a country Baptist church north of Vidalia in rural Toombs County. "I've seen the church, and I think I know why they picked it for the service. It's just a little off the way between Statesboro and Vidalia. One weekend when I went home from college with Mindy, she said she wanted to show me something. So we turned off the main highway and rode for miles until we came to this crossroads. It was in the middle of nowhere and surrounded by fields and farmland, but right there was this beautiful church that sat in a grove of old oak trees. Mindy told me, 'This is where I want to get married.'"

The church, Mount Moriah Missionary Baptist, was at the heart of a rural farming settlement when it was constructed more than a century earlier. With time and the demise of family farms, the area's population dwindled but the church and its loyal congregation remained. It had been at this church where Mindy's parents first met as teenagers, a relationship that led to marriage and two children. When they were young, the family often attended services there. "I guess Mindy told her mother about wanting to have a wedding there, and maybe that's why Mrs. Davis chose the site."

"Okay," I said, trying to hide the fact I was not eager to go.

"I can't imagine there'll be many people there. It's not a huge church, and it's a long way from everywhere. But I'll go—no, we'll go—and then have...," she paused a brief moment, "...closure."

The memorial service was scheduled for a Friday afternoon at 4:00 p.m., an unusual time, I thought, and in such a rural location that I didn't expect many to show up. A small, discreet notice of the service had appeared in both the Statesboro and Toombs County papers, and I later learned that the local Fox affiliate television station in Savannah had run a short segment on the discovery of the body and the planned service, which I presumed was open to the public. Unusually for late summer, the day was beautiful. A low pressure front bringing slightly cooler weather had blown through earlier in the week, cleansing the air with rain, and resulting in cooler temperatures with a perfectly blue sky on that Friday. Jenna, not precisely sure how to reach the church, insisted that we leave early. I pointed out that we had Google maps and GPS navigation, but she was insistent. She dressed demurely in a dark green dress. I wore a blue sport coat without a tie.

As I suspected, we arrived at the church nearly forty-five minutes early. It was indeed a beautiful setting, the ancient oaks surrounding the white wooden church with its slim steeple pointing toward the clear sky. The paved parking lot, set to one side of the structure, was unusually large given the isolated location. An older Ford sedan was parked in front of a slot labeled "Reserved for Minister," while an employee of a Vidalia florist carried several loads of flowers into the sanctuary. We parked in the shade on the edge of the lot, waiting until closer to the appointed hour to enter the church. Fifteen minutes later, a nondescript gray van with deeply tinted windows drove slowly in, circled about the lot for a few minutes as if looking for a place to park, then chose a spot near the front entry walkway. I commented to Jenna that they were likely to get pulled over by the cops with that much window tint; she responded with a disinterested, "Hmm."

As the lot began to fill up with cars and the occasional pickup, a trickle of people began to enter the church about twenty minutes before the hour. Eying them intently, Jenna said she wanted to wait until the last minute to go—she didn't want to have "too many emotional conversations." I asked if she thought there would be people here that she knew besides Mindy's family. She replied with a terse, "Probably." At 3:55, we got out of my car and headed toward the church's entrance. As we drew nearer, I noticed two men get out of the gray van and head up the sidewalk just in front of us. Both appeared to be in their late thirties or early forties, well-dressed in long-sleeved shirts, but no coat or tie. For some reason, they seemed out of place. I started to mention this to Jenna, but she seemed in an emotional turmoil, with clenched teeth and a fixed expression on her normally beautiful face.

Inside, the church interior was lined with unpainted pine darkened with age, and softly illuminated from the glow of stained glass windows on either side. As our eyes adjusted to the change, it was clear that the sanctuary was mostly full, with well in excess of a hundred people in attendance. An usher seated us on a back row near the entrance. An organist began to play softly; I didn't recognize the tune, but it sounded reasonably mournful. The minister, who had been seated adjacent to the pulpit in the front, rose and welcomed us to "this sad occasion." He offered up a prayer, after which Mindy's brother, now a cardiologist practicing in Savannah, spoke, praising his "wonderful, quirky, life-loving" sibling, and bemoaning her death. The congregation then stood and sang a hymn on "life eternal," followed by another longish prayer and benediction. The minister announced that "refreshments" were available in the adjacent social hall, and that the family would be there "to receive us." It was all very Southern.

We adjourned to the social hall, basically a large room with an attached kitchen. Mindy's mother, her son Peter and other members of the family stood in a receiving line, speaking quietly with a long row of those paying their respects. Jenna seemed reluctant. "We have to do this," I told her as we joined the queue. Both Peter and Mrs. Davis hugged Jenna, who by this time was crying without embarrassment. I stood quietly by, my hand on her shoulder, nodding as I was introduced. Looking about, I observed the two men who had arrived in the gray van standing quietly to one side, closely observing the room. Something here was out of place, I thought, but quickly turned my attention back to Jenna.

Having made our way through the line, Jenna grabbed my hand and said, "Let's go, please. I don't know if I can take any more of this." She pulled me in the direction of the exit. As we worked our way through the crowd, past the buffet line and the tables loaded with food, a middle-aged man dressed in a well-pressed work shirt looked at Jenna, smiled and stuck out his hand. "I know you, don't I?" he asked, incongruously.

"I think not," Jenna said, tugging even more urgently on my hand.

"Wait, I do. You were Mindy's friend, weren't you?"

"Yes, we were friends from college," Jenna replied, our escape route temporally blocked by a woman bringing another tray of pimento cheese sandwiches to the table.

"No, it must have been after that, I guess. Didn't you work with Mindy at the club in Savannah?" Jenna's face blanched. The man continued, "I remember now…, you're Candi, you and Mindy used to…." His sentence was cut short as Jenna slapped him forcefully, then pushed her way toward the door.

CHAPTER 11

Jenna was livid. The slap, which seemed to echo off the walls of the social hall, brought conversation to an abrupt halt in the room, followed by a sudden quiet. All eyes turned in our direction as she grabbed my hand and rushed toward the door and the freedom of the parking lot. Once safely in my car Jenna sat silently, her jaw clenched and her arms folded tightly over her chest. I started to speak, but thought better of it. "I knew I shouldn't have come," she said, a note of bitterness in her voice.

"I'm sorry...," I said, only to be cut off by Jenna as she stared straight ahead.

"There's something wrong with this whole scene," she continued, ignoring me. "They invited the public. Anybody could show up. And those two guys...," she turned toward me, "...did you see them, John? The ones that got out of the gray van. They just stood around and watched the crowd. They didn't speak to the family or anyone else so far as I could see. I think they were cops. You learn to spot them when you work in a club like I did with Mindy." She stopped for a moment, still staring intently ahead at nothing in particular.

"Like I started to say," I began, "I told you to come and...."

"And the cameras in the church and social hall." Jenna interrupted me again. I had noticed several video cameras scattered about, thinking that this church, like many others, streamed their services online for the benefit of those who could not attend worship. "The members of this church are mostly hard-shell, old school Baptists," Jenna continued. "They are not about to let somebody off the hook for attending church with the excuse that they listened to the preacher's sermon from home. I grew up just a couple of counties over from here. I know how that is. They were filming the crowd, seeing who'd show up for the service." She was quiet once again.

Just at that moment, the two men she'd referred to walked out of the church, climbed back into the gray van and drove away. Jenna eyed it suspiciously. "See those tinted windows? That's a surveillance van. I guarantee you there's a couple of other guys sitting behind them and taking photos of who showed up. And why did Mrs. Davis call and tell me how much she wanted me to be there? Was it because Mindy and I were close friends at one time, or have the investigators gotten the idea that I'm somehow connected with her murder? I was in rehab when she went missing, and didn't even know about it for the longest time."

The idea flashed through my thoughts that Jenna was becoming a bit paranoid. The stress surrounding the discovery of Mindy's remains, the guy in the social hall who recognized her from a past she was ashamed of, the uncertainty of what the future might reveal; all had to weigh heavily upon her. I wanted so much to reach out, to put my arms around her and assure her that I would be there for her. If I could have, I would have in that very moment, but it had become clear that what seemed to stand between an uncertain present and an unknown future were answers to questions yet to be asked, and past events yet to be understood.

We drove back to Claxton mostly in silence, stopping only at the drive-thru of the local McDonald's to get a vanilla milkshake for Jenna. I tried making conversation, thinking perhaps it might take her mind off the events of the afternoon. I tried telling her in so many words that I had her back, that she could count on me for support no matter what. Lost in her own thoughts, she responded only with fleeting expressions of appreciation, leaving me unsure that she either believed me or fully understood what I was trying to say. It was dusk when we reached her apartment. She thanked me briefly and disappeared inside, saying she would call or text over the weekend.

Saturday passed without any word from Jenna. I tried to pretend that everything was fine; she was just going through a rough patch. I suppressed the urge to call her or check my phone to be sure I hadn't missed her call. She finally got in touch late Sunday afternoon, spending the first minutes of our conversation apologizing for the way she acted at the memorial service. "I was just upset. There were too many memories, too many flashbacks to situations and places and people. I hope I'm better now." I mumbled a few words of encouragement before she continued. "But, John, the one thing that I cannot get out of my mind is this: what happened to Mindy could have happened to me. The other day when I called to asked you whether or not I should go to the service, and you stuck your foot in your mouth talking about 'a girl with a bright future who ended up on drugs and working as a stripper in a bar'—that's me. Or that *was* me. So, I want to know why. Why her? Why not me? Was it just whatever they call fate—like someone who gets caught in traffic on their way to the airport and misses the plane and then learns that everyone on board was killed when it crashed? I almost feel guilty, like maybe that should have been me, and Mindy was a second choice."

"I understand, or think I understand," I said. "I just want you to remember that I care about you, and will do whatever I need to do to help you get through this."

"I know that," Jenna replied. "There is one thing that I'd like you to do for me. For the last couple of days—ever since we left the service Friday afternoon—I've wanted some kind of answer to those 'why' questions. I want to know more about the details of Mindy's death. Was she murdered, and did she suffer? Or maybe there was an accident, or she OD'ed on some new drug and whoever she was with got scared and hid her body? I want to know what happened, and if that's not possible, I want someone to tell me we can never know and I'll have to be content with that."

I wasn't sure how to answer her. "Jenna, I'm sure those are the same questions the investigators want to know. If what you said was true about the cameras and the two guys and the van with the tinted windows, it would appear that they are actively pursuing the answers. And I am absolutely sure they're not about to share anything with me. These things take time and sometimes they never…."

"I understand all that," she said. "But I just want some assurance that they are chasing every possible lead." She hesitated. "And you remember what I said about Mindy's mother calling to especially invite me? She had to know the police would be there. They must know I was Mindy's friend, but they haven't tried to interview me. Why not?"

"I feel certain they'll get to you at some point if necessary, but I think the most likely answer is that they don't see any reason right now to do so. If they have leads, they don't involve you." I didn't accuse Jenna of paranoia, but once again she was sounding that way.

"You're probably right," she replied. "But still…."

"What exactly do you want me to do?" I said, trying to redirect the conversation.

"You have connections. You know people, or you know people who have connections. I want to find out what happened to Mindy, at least as much as can be known. I want to know if they have any hopes of finding her killer, or if she wasn't murdered, or how she died and why someone hid her body."

"Jenna, I think I'd be correct to say that this is what they call a cold case. Mindy went missing years ago. Everyone had to assume something happened to her, and that included the strong probability that she was no longer alive. I can't say any more than that, but I think it's very unlikely that the Georgia Bureau of Investigation or whichever agency is in charge, is going to share their knowledge with me. So…."

"But if they're calling it a cold case, wouldn't they want any help they could get? I'd be happy to speak with them, to tell them what I know."

"What do you know that they may not be aware of?"

Jenna didn't respond immediately, then, "Probably nothing…."

"Do you want me to make some inquiries, maybe ask if they'd like to interview you?"

"You can, but you also have friends in law enforcement. Ask them what they know or can find out. And your friend the lawyer, Phil Holloway, doesn't he specialize in criminal defense? He might know something, or I'm sure he would have friends…."

"Okay," I said, cutting her off. "I'll look into things for you."

"Thank you," Jenna said, once again hanging up without saying good-bye.

CHAPTER 12

While I'd given a positive answer to Jenna, agreeing to make some inquiries, it seemed to be one of those situations with no good outcome. The likely scenario would be that all doors would be slammed in my face, citing "an ongoing investigation," law enforcement's (and politicians') favorite excuse to avoid answering questions. Any way I could imagine it, common sense pointed at disappointment, and since I had agreed to do the task, the blame would fall on me, possibly delivering a mortal blow to my relationship with Jenna. From that viewpoint, this could become a do or die situation. I recalled visiting my grandparents in Savannah when I was a small child, perhaps five years old. It was mid-summer, and my grandfather had taken me for a walk in Forsyth Park. We were strolling along, my hand in his when I saw something move in one of the flower beds. Breaking away, I rushed over to see that the object was a black snake, one I later learned was a highly poisonous cottonmouth moccasin. I was reaching out to try to grab it just as my grandfather scooped me up and quickly moved me out of danger. "One thing you need to remember, son, is this. Don't ever mess with something that can bite you," he said. I thought about that on Monday morning as I picked up the phone to call Phil Holloway.

Phil is a highly respected attorney, a partner in the firm of Randolph, Holloway & Lamar, LLP, and the bane of prosecutors when defending clients accused of a wide variety of crimes. Having helped me through several bad situations, he had become a trusted friend and advisor, usually the first person I'd call for thorny problems of all sorts, both legal and otherwise.

His secretary put me straight through. "What's up this time, John? Don't tell me you've gotten in hot water again," Phil asked, half laughing.

"No," I explained. "Just trying to help out my friend, Jenna."

"Well, I hope she doesn't need a lawyer…?"

"No, nothing at all like that." I briefly explained about the chance discovery of the remains of her close friend Mindy, and Jenna's desire to know the status of the investigation.

"I know how you feel about Jenna, and maybe I shouldn't even ask this, but is there a chance she's somehow involved in the girl's death?" Phil asked. It bothered me to think that was the first thing that came to his mind.

"No, there's nothing to suggest that. She was, er…, away when Mindy disappeared, and said she didn't know until much later that she was even missing." I didn't want to have to explain that Jenna was in court-mandated rehab at the time.

"So, what do you want from me?" Phil asked.

"It's not what I want, Phil, it's what Jenna wants to know. Even though they'd grown apart, they were best friends in college, and reconnected later. They worked together for a good while in Savannah." I didn't say where. "I mean she knew Mindy was missing and all, and I guess she and everyone else assumed the worse, but never knew the truth until they found her skeleton buried somewhere in the countryside just off I-16. We went to the memorial service last week in Toombs County, and I think Jenna seeing Mindy's mother and brother, and other people she knew, opened old wounds."

"Oh," Phil said. "Seeking closure, I guess."

"Something like that, yeah." I silently swore never again to use the word 'closure.'

"Okay, let me do this. I'll make a few phone calls and see what I can find out. I'll start with the GBI, because this appears to be multijurisdictional and it's probable that they're coordinating the case. I have some friends there and I'm pretty sure I can get the basics about what's going on. Let's start with that, and make plans about going forward after we know where the investigation stands."

I thanked him, hung up and immediately called Jenna. I told her what I had done, and of Phil's willingness to find out the status of the case and hopefully get us started in the right direction. "You're wonderful, John." She paused. "Listen, I know this is short notice, but Robert is off at church camp for a few days and I'm by myself. Can I come and spend the night at your place tonight?"

I smiled. "Yes, of course. I'd like that very much."

The remainder of my week was pleasant. I did not hear from Phil Holloway until late Thursday afternoon. He apologized for the delay, and set out to tell me what he had discovered.

"I got ahold of my friend there at the GBI, and ended up talking with several other folks. The case is being handled out of the GBI's Region 5 office in Statesboro, and the examination of the victim's remains was done at the State Crime Lab in Savannah, plus some DNA analysis they'd outsourced. It seems the ID of Mary Nelle Davis—you called her Mindy—is well established, so that's a given. She was reported as a missing person a number of years ago as you know. The GBI was only peripherally involved in that; back then most of the investigation was handled by the Savannah/Chatham County cops. The body was found in south Bulloch County, and no one seems to have any idea of whether there's a connection there or not."

Holloway paused and I could hear papers shuffling. "It seems," he began, "that Mindy was working as a waitress and possibly as a dancer at a club south of Savannah. On talking to the guy with the Savannah cops who worked the case, they didn't delve into that aspect too much. Miss Mindy apparently came from a prominent family in Vidalia, and when they tried to find out what she'd been up to—you know, drugs, maybe prostitution—everyone clammed up. One guy I was talking to there said the mother reacted with something like, 'How dare you accuse my daughter of such,' so they didn't get into it, and nobody in the club or bar or whatever it was wanted to talk. It's like she went home one Saturday and was never seen or heard from again until someone stumbled on her bones forty-something miles away in the middle of nowhere."

"Not much help, then," I observed.

"Well, yeah. But a large part of the problem is that they did a half-assed investigation after she went missing, and now years later don't know where to start. I talked to one of the Savannah cops who was in on the case—he's retired now. He said 'We just figured she'd run off with some man, and would show back up when she'd had enough of him.'"

I saw an opening for Jenna. "Jenna was not there when Mindy went missing, but she was working there around that time. She might have some information, or shed some light on things. As I said, she had been pretty close to Mindy since they were in college together. She said Mindy had gotten on drugs."

"Yeah. The cops knew that and—this is me reading between the lines here—that's probably one of the reasons they didn't push the investigation harder. 'Just another addict breaking the law, so why waste our time?'" Phil paused, then, "Bastards."

"Should I say something to Jenna about offering to tell the GBI what she knows?"

"I would think so, but give me a few more days to do some digging. There are still several people I want to talk with. Everything I've heard about what the Crime Lab found is secondhand. There's someone there who will speak to me off the record, I'm sure, but she's been out of town at a conference. I hope she'll be available next week. Maybe I can help you two think through the options after that."

"It's Jenna, not me," I reminded Phil.

"At this point, John, I think you two are part of each other's lives whether you recognize it or not."

I wasn't sure how to respond, so I said nothing.

CHAPTER 13

It was mid-week before I heard back from Holloway. He said the conversation with his contact at the Crime Lab was most interesting. By way of background, he explained, even though they're doing vital work that directly impacts both specific cases and law enforcement in general, most of the people who work there "don't have the mindset of a cop," to quote him. In other words, the cop on the street or the homicide detective, for example, sees horror, depravity, gore, and plain human cruelty on a regular and continuing basis. Their thoughts and re actions are shaped by recurring exposure and near daily interaction with the worst of the human species. The crime lab folks, though, come across as detached, less emotional and more cerebral in viewing the same situations and sets of facts. "And in addition to that," Holloway continued, "they usually know a hell of a lot more about looking for the details that win or lose convictions in court." He was convinced his contact, a woman whom he would describe only as "a friend for many years," was willing to share with him everything she knew. I didn't press him for details.

Holloway had managed to get a look at a copy of the crime lab report, most of which detailed the examination of the site where Mindy's skeletal remains were found, and examination of the skeleton itself. It appeared the body had originally been buried no more than two feet below the surface of the earth, with the part that attracted discovery revealed by erosion from heavy winter and early spring rains. Other than the jewelry, there was nothing to indicate the victim had been clothed when buried. In a comments section it was noted that such items as shoes, belts, plastic objects like buttons, and clothing made of polyester were highly resistant to decay, but no such evidence was found. The report contained two important bits of information that were new to me. Two facial bones, the zygoma and the maxilla, making up the lower and lateral borders of the right eye socket had been recently broken, suggesting that Mindy had been beaten at or near the time of her death. As they were both on her right side, the report also suggested that a left-handed individual may have inflicted these wounds. In addition to these, her hyoid bone, the small, U-shaped bone in the anterior neck just above the larynx, had been broken as well, strongly suggesting strangulation as a primary cause of death. The remainder of the report briefly outlined the circumstances that led to the discovery of the remains, but avoided any speculation or inference otherwise.

"So, not a lot there," I said to Holloway.

"Maybe yes and maybe no. I haven't had the onerous task of trying to defend someone for a murder as brutal as this, but my first reaction is that we just learned a lot about the killer. Back off for a minute and look at what little we know. First, there's the victim. She's female, into drugs, and maybe even making a few bucks on the side as an escort. In that role, she's one of society's most vulnerable citizens. And even though the lab couldn't do a proper autopsy on what was found, you know pretty well that she was beaten and strangled, a painful and horrific way to die. That immediately brings up two possible motives—among many of course. The person that did this—I'd presume it was a guy—was either angry with her, or angry with what she represented to him. Say Mindy was this guy's girlfriend. He finds out she's been cheating on him, or turning tricks to earn a little cash. They're both drinking, he's pretty drunk and they get in a fight. He beats the crap out of her and when she fights back, he starts strangling her. And then as he begins to come to his senses, realizes she's stopped breathing. So, he panics and tries to dispose of the body. And something else on top of that: the crime lab folks believe she was naked when she was buried. That makes you think her killing was what the cops like to call a 'sex crime,' which can mean about anything. Or alternatively, some sick dude has a problem with his mother, or certain types of young women—I don't know. He lures Mindy out and transfers his anger to her."

Holloway paused, catching his breath before continuing. "And then there are serial killers, the kind who get some perverted pleasure out of beating and raping and strangling women. Do you remember hearing about that guy that killed the elderly women over in Columbus back in the late '70s—the 'Stocking Strangler,' they called him? That sort. As I recall, there were seven or eight victims. But the thing is, he got away with it, at least for a while. The cops were all over the place, doing everything possible to catch him, but the killings stopped and the case went cold. And it was a bit of luck involving a totally unrelated case that eventually led to the killer's arrest years later. This could be that kind of situation. You just never know what…."

"I understand," I said, interrupting him. "I think you've made it clear that even knowing where to start is the first major problem. Let me do this: I'll talk with Jenna and see if she really wants to get involved in this case, in this search. It's beginning to sound like doing so would be taking the lid off Pandora's box. I didn't realize how close she was to Mindy. It seems the more we learn—the more we know—the worse it gets. I'm hoping I can convince her to let the proper people, the proper agencies, finish their investigation."

"A very good idea, I'd say," Holloway replied.

I called Jenna and told her it would be a couple of days before I heard from several folks I wanted to talk with. That wasn't exactly correct. The truth was, I needed to think about the situation and plot a course of action. There were plenty of facts, or things presented as such, but in the end I realized I didn't know a lot. Part of that was because this was originally a missing person case that had been sloppily investigated with little apparent follow up. The crime lab's current analysis was no doubt well done, but due to the time that had elapsed, there were things that were impossible to determine, such as DNA evidence that could point to her killer, or whether drugs might have played a role in Mindy's death. Why was her body found in Bulloch County when she lived and worked in Savannah? Assuming the crime lab assessment was correct, why was she naked when her body was buried? And was the memorial service held in part to see who would show up, or was there another explanation for the van with tinted windows and the two out-of-place guys who seemed more interested in the crowd than Mindy's family? Most importantly, I had no idea about which direction the current investigation was taking. The crime had happened years earlier. Potential suspects or witnesses would have been scattered by time, and the details of events surrounding Mindy's disappearance faded from collective memories. I came to what I decided was the most logical of all possible conclusions: Jenna should volunteer to give assistance to the investigators if wanted or needed, but otherwise it would be best for her to back off, letting those charged with solving crimes do their best to solve this one, if possible.

What, if anything, Jenna should do, and how much I should assist her or otherwise get involved, had become a hot-button issue. As long as I had known her, as long as we had been involved as more than friends, I had never seen this side of her. Before we met she had hit bottom and survived, emerging as a strong, forthright friend and lover. Perhaps I was overreacting to her seeming fixation on the investigation of the death of a former close friend. In Madrid, I had come within minutes of asking her to spend the rest of her life with me as my wife. In a city full of beautiful and romantic settings, if I had chosen somewhere else to offer her my love and a ring, we would have been married by now. How would I have handled this crisis? I had no idea, but reasoned that she had done nothing to make me rethink my love for her. I would follow her wishes, even knowing that we might both regret the outcome.

I glanced at my watch. It was just past six-thirty in the evening. Jenna would be home, and Robert probably doing his homework or playing videogames. I called. "Hey," Jenna said, sounding happy to hear my voice. "Did you have a good day?"

"Yes, and I wanted to go over what I've learned about the investigation."

"Okay…," she said, a sudden change in the tone of her voice.

For the next ten minutes I recounted what I'd learned, explaining the obvious fact that in retrospect the investigation after Mindy's disappearance was neither intensive nor especially detailed. The state crime lab examination of her remains appeared to have been well done, but there was not a lot to work with, and no important clues were found to reveal the details of her death or who might be responsible. As to the reopened investigation, "I wasn't able to find out much at all," I explained. "Phil Holloway spoke with his contacts in the GBI, and a retired Savannah detective who was on the case when Mindy first went missing. He didn't hear about any great breakthroughs or new leads. My impression is that her murder is still a cold case."

There was silence on the other end of the line. Then, "I want to know what happened, John. I want us to do whatever it takes to find out."

CHAPTER 14

I told Jenna that I would try, and flopped down on the couch in my apartment struggling to decide what to do next. Strangely, the first thought that came to mind was Jenna's description of the night she was arrested for DUI and possession. She said she had fallen asleep while driving home, drifted off the highway and found herself in kind of a ditch, unable to get back on the road. That seemed to be an appropriate analogy for my current situation. My carefully laid plans, my goals, and my future lay somewhere down the road, while I seemed to be mired in the ditch carved by memories of someone else's past. This had to change.

After tossing various options back and forth, I decided to call Pete Marsh. A detective with the Savannah police, we had met more than a year earlier when he was working with the homicide division on a case that involved the murder of one of my art gallery's clients. In large part because of his work on that situation, he had been promoted to head of the Homicide Division. At the time of her disappearance, Mindy Davis was living in Savannah. According to Phil Holloway, the local cops took part in the initial investigation, so there was a good chance that Pete would be willing to help. I pulled up the contact list on my phone and tapped the number for his cell. He answered almost immediately with a friendly, "John, how are you? Your name popped up with your number."

"I'm doing well, thanks. I've got a bit of a situation, and I'd like to get your advice."

"Sure," Pete said, a note of concern in his voice. "Nothing serious, I hope."

"No, I don't think so. It's about a cold case that tangentially involves my friend, Jenna."

"Are you talking about the Mindy Davis thing? Your attorney was calling around the other day looking for information. I didn't want to talk with him because I didn't know why he was asking. Were you behind that?"

"Not directly," I said, "but it's a little complicated. Mindy was Jenna's close friend, and wants to know what happened."

"Oh," Pete said, then continued, "She's not involved in any way, I hope?"

"No, not at all," I said. Like Holloway, Pete seemed immediately suspicious of why she would be asking questions.

"Well, that's good. This is still an open case, and because the Davis girl was a resident of Savannah when she first disappeared, we headed up the investigation. There'd been no leads for years until recently—I guess you already know that." He paused, then, "So, how can I be of help to you?"

"It's kind of a long story, complicated and kind of personal. I think it would be easier to talk in person when you have time."

"Any time is fine with me. Want to get together later this afternoon?" We agreed to meet at 5:30 at a quiet tavern on Abercorn near the mall.

I arrived on time to find Pete already there, sitting in a quiet corner booth nursing a beer. He flashed a genuine smile and said, "It's good to see you, John. Sit down and tell me what's going on."

I ordered coffee, and started the narrative with the call to Jenna from Mindy's mother, ending nearly fifteen minutes later with, "...and that's why I'm here. Jenna wants to know what happened."

Pete took a sip on his beer and said, "Let me tell you where things stand from our end." The Savannah police have a cold case unit, he explained, and more recently a cold case unit was created within the Chatham County District Attorney's office. Both could be credited with some successes, but a number of murders and related crimes from years past remained unsolved. "This Mindy girl was a dancer, a druggie, and probably trading a little sex for cash every now and then. She went missing not long after I joined the force here. From what I recall, there was an investigation, but with no ready clues as to what had happened, it got put on the back burner. It was never officially turned over to the cold case group, mainly due to the total lack of leads. When they found her body—or what was left of it—several months ago, the GBI called and asked us to get back on the case, and that's where I came in because it had now transitioned from a missing person situation to a murder investigation. Both the Bureau and the local homicide guys reviewed the files, followed up on some interviews, and so on, but it wasn't long before the file was back on the shelf. Right now, so far as I know, the investigation has come to a standstill. Without further leads, new information, new witnesses and the like, we don't know what more we can do." Pete swallowed a long draught of his beer. "That's about it. Right now it looks like someone has gotten away with murder."

"Okay, it's good to know where things stand," I said, "but let me ask you a couple of specific questions. There was a memorial service held a couple of weeks ago. There was a out-of-place gray van with tinted windows there, and a couple of guys who Jenna thought were cops. Were they your guys?"

"I hate to admit it, but yeah. A few weeks after they found the girl's remains, there was something in the paper about a memorial service held over in Toombs County. One of the guys, I forget who, saw something in the paper and had the bright idea of sending a crew from the force to take photos, to monitor things, the thought being that sometimes killers will show up at services for their victims. It's crazy, I know, but we didn't have anything to lose except for the cost of a little extra overtime pay for the two guys and the tech in the back of the van with a camera. To make a long story short, nothing came of it. Nothing suspicious happened, and the photos—we identified about twenty individuals we wanted to check out—yielded nothing. Everybody there had a reason to be there—you know, relatives, friends of Mindy or friends of the family, people she'd known in school or college, several old teachers, that sort."

"Jenna said the guys were cops and the cameras were filming who was there," I said.

"Smart girl," Pete replied. "I'll pass that on. They need to be less obvious next time. You said you had a couple of questions. What was the second one?"

"I think you've answered it. Since Mindy's mother especially invited her, and of course had to know the cops would be there screening people, Jenna was worried that she might be a suspect. I take it that's not the case…?"

Pete laughed. "No, not at all. Mrs. Davis mentioned to us that Jenna and Mindy were close friends. That's why she wanted her there."

"That will be a relief, I'm sure…," I began.

"But you always have to remember the old saying, 'The hit dog hollers.'" Pete said. 'You'd be surprised how true that is in murder investigations."

“Yeah, sounds like something my grandfather would say,” I said, thinking of how he had saved me from being bitten by the moccasin when I was a young child.

I visited for a while longer with Pete, each of us catching up on what the other had been doing. I told him the gallery was doing extremely well, and about my trip to Spain with Jenna. “You wouldn’t be thinking about you two getting married now, would you?” he asked.

“The idea had crossed my mind, yeah.”

“That’s great. I only met her when she was with you and don’t know her well, but she seems like a wonderful person.”

“She is, and between me and you, I’ve been seriously thinking about asking her to marry me. I’ve even gotten a ring. But she’s taking this thing with Mindy real hard. She’s almost obsessive in wanting to know what happened, and I’m sure it would be hard to talk about marriage until the investigation comes to some end, one way or the other. It’s like someone has dumped a bucket of cold water on my plans.” I was silent for a few seconds, wondering if I should say more. Pete seemed to be waiting for me to continue. “Listen,” I said, “I know this may sound a little crazy, but can I help with things, maybe assist the department with the case in some way? I can do research, reread the old case reports to see if there’s something that’s been missed, chase down leads, or whatever....”

Pete stared at his beer for a moment, then said, “Well, you are a lawyer....”

“Was a lawyer, remember? I was disbarred.”

“That was totally political, in case you’ve forgotten. You were screwed. You know you could reapply and be reinstated in a minute.”

"That's probably true, but it's not what I want to do at this point in my life. I want to live a quiet life, run the gallery, maybe marry Jenna if she'll have me…."

"And you say this sort of hinges on getting the Davis case to some resolution? It's looking now like her killer will never be found, so what are you going to do, sit around and wait until your old age…? For god's sake, John, you've had a pretty rough time of things for the last several years. Isn't it time you found some happiness? Look, if you think your working to help find an end to this case will change your future for the better, let's do it. I'll run your offer by the powers-that-be at the department and see what I can do. After what you've been through, we owe you one."

CHAPTER 15

The more I thought about Pete Marsh's offer, the more it appealed to me. If he was able to somehow get me directly involved in the investigation of Mindy's death, it would present an ideal chance to wrap things up and move on. Realistically speaking, I'd be foolish to think her killer would be found or her case resolved in some way; hundreds of eyes had poured over the known facts and evidence originally, and again recently when the search was reopened. But, I would presumably have access to everything known by the investigators, could draw my own conclusions about the thoroughness of the search, and legitimately make suggestions for other routes of inquiry. Most importantly to me, it would avoid direct involvement by Jenna, and the certain emotional turmoil that would produce. She would trust me, I hoped, and if—or more likely, when—things came to the inevitable conclusion that nothing more could be done to solve the case, she could move on with her life. We could move on together.

I let Jenna know that I'd met with Pete Marsh, but didn't go into any details, vaguely explaining that he was looking into some options that might let us have some input into the search. She seemed satisfied. Three days passed before I heard from Pete. This whole tragedy, the senseless murder of someone I had never met, hung over my days like a dark cloud. Just as I would get involved in something at the gallery, or attempt to read a book, or try to fall asleep at night, it would barge back into my consciousness, the psychic equivalent of a pain that won't go away.

Pete's call seemed to break the spell. "I've spoken with several people at headquarters, including the chief and most of the members of the cold case unit. They had questions—lots of them in fact—but they're willing to consider adding you on as an investigator. You'd be a sworn officer, but with limited duties and privileges relating only to this case. And you wouldn't be paid, of course." I heard him take a deep breath on the other end of the line. "Look, John, normally everyone up and down the command chain would say 'Hell, no!' but I pointed out to them that we knew you pretty well from that screw-up last year with the Moule murder, and your only agenda was to help out your fiancée, who had been close friends with the victim—I hope you didn't mind my referring to Jenna like that. The real kicker, though, the one thing that pushed them to consider you, is the fact that they've made little or no progress on solving this crime. For all the time and effort and money that several law enforcement agencies have spent on this case, about the only thing we can be certain about is that we have a dead woman who obviously was murdered. Before we go any further, let me ask you this: Are you sure you want to get involved? I ask that because you're smart, educated, and don't like to fail."

"Yes, it's what I want to do."

"Okay, then. Can you meet me at headquarters sometime this week? The chief and several of the guys want to interview you before they make a final decision."

"Just let me know when…."

"I'll be in touch, then," Pete said and hung up.

Jenna and I had a date planned for the evening. The timing had nothing to do with "the Mindy thing," as I'd come to privately refer to it, but rather had been planned earlier to celebrate her birthday. I made reservations at The Mansion on Forsyth Park, offering a near-perfect combination of an eclectic menu billed as "contemporary Italian," great atmosphere, and a good wine cellar. She drove over from Claxton, planning to spend the night. As her gift, I had found an antique coin-silver bracelet set with a single green emerald. I wanted to present the possibility of my working directly with the Savannah police on my terms, but I knew it would be the first thing she asked about. I suggested we discuss it over drinks before dinner. Remembering our time in Madrid, I ordered a good bottle of Spanish cava, and waited until we had mostly finished the second glass to bring up the subject.

"I talked with Pete Marsh…," I began, watching as Jenna set her glass on the table and leaned forward, eager to hear the plans. I explained that he suggested I work as a deputized investigator but on this case only. It would be somewhat of an unusual arrangement, but justified primarily because the first investigation and the more recent one after the discovery of Mindy's remains had gotten nowhere. The important thing, though, was that with me in that position, she would probably not have to undergo a police interview—I could pass on whatever new information she had that might be helpful. Jenna stood up, walked around to my side of the table, leaned over and kissed me, much to the amusement of the other diners. "I love you, John O'Toole," she said.

I spent several hours over the next few days being interviewed by various members of the Savannah/Chatham County police force. Some officers were friendlier than others and several were clearly suspicious of my motives, but in the end, all went well. Pete called to say that while my position was a unique one, I had the backing of the department and could look forward to their full cooperation. "So, when do you want to get started?" I told him I'd need a few days to make arrangements to be away from work, but I thought I could start the following week.

"Okay," Pete said, "but I think the first thing you need to do is see what material is available—get a first look at the investigation files and that sort of thing. And I want a friend of mine—he's retired now—to see if he can get you started in the right direction. Let's plan on that for the first couple of days, and then you'll be on your own. I'm here—we're here—to help or answer questions any time, but I promise we won't get in your way."

Bright and early on a beautiful September morning I walked from my Liberty Street home the few short blocks to police headquarters, ready to begin my adventure. In truth, I had no idea what to expect, but had packed a small satchel with a bound notebook, pens, an iPad if I needed to consult the internet, and several legal pads to scribble notes. Instead of getting an immediate start, I spent the next three hours being formally sworn in as an "investigator," having my photo taken—for an ID, they told me—and listening to a very pleasant lady from Human Resources deliver a long list of "do's and don'ts."

Pete took me to lunch, after which he led me to a small brightly-lit windowless room tucked away on the third floor of the old building, a former police barracks. The plan, he explained, was to give me the remainder of the day, and all day the next, to sift through the case files on my own—"to get a feel for the lay of the land" as he termed it. On the third day, he would schedule a meeting with his friend, a now-retired homicide detective, to give me a few pointers. He wished me good luck and told me to call if I needed anything. A few minutes later, an efficient-looking older lady pushed in a large cart stacked with cardboard bankers boxes numbered 1 through 6, each packed with files in manila folders. She handed me a loose-leafed ring binder. "This is all we've got on the Davis case," she said. "A lot of this is digitized, but I've found most people want to look at the original files. And this," she said, tapping on the binder, "is the directory. It's much easier to look up things here than trying to do so on a computer. If you need any help, I'm just down the hall." With that, she smiled and left, shutting the door behind her.

I looked around the room. It was totally bare except for a moderate-sized work table and two chairs. A large whiteboard hung on the wall opposite the entry door. Video cameras were mounted near the ceiling at each end of the room providing coverage of every inch. I wondered if I was being recorded. I laid the directory on the table in front of me and began flipping through the pages, surveying what secrets the boxes contained. Of the six boxes, the first four held documents from the initial investigation. Numbers 5 and 6 pertained to material collected since the more recent discovery of Mindy's remains. I estimated each box could easily hold ten 500-sheet reams of paper. The files within the boxes appeared to be packed tightly, so the six boxes might contain 30,000 pages or more of documents pertaining to the case.

I wasn't sure where to start, and for a moment felt overwhelmed. Turning back to the directory, I ran my finger down the list of files for the first page of Box 1. Near the top, a title caught my eye. It read "Photos of Victim—From Family." Curious, I hefted the box off the cart and on to the table. Checking the directory again to be sure I had the correct number, I pulled out a thick manila folder packed with photographs of varying sizes. At that moment, I realized I had no idea what Mindy looked like. As many times as Jenna and I had discussed her, the subject of her exact appearance had never been mentioned. I had never seen a photo of her. I vaguely had the idea that she might have been a blonde, but then Jenna was blonde so maybe I had just assumed her close friend would resemble her.

The first image I pulled from the folder was a group of half a dozen high school cheerleaders. I flipped it over. There was nothing written on the back to indicate who was who. Next I pulled out what appeared to be an elementary school yearbook photo of a young blond girl, perhaps six or eight years old. I assumed this was Mindy, but obviously she would have appeared quite different as an adult. Reaching in again, I withdrew a larger eight-by-ten studio photo of a strikingly beautiful young woman with blue eyes and shoulder-length blond hair. On the back, an ink inscription read "Mary Nelle Davis, Senior Photo, Georgia Southern University." I stared at it, perhaps shocked would have been the best way to describe my reaction. Even though she was younger, the image of Mindy Davis in the photo bore a striking resemblance to Jenna.

CHAPTER 16

Ever since I first heard from Jenna of Mindy going missing, or later when news came of the discovery of her remains, her disappearance and death had been abstract concepts with the limited emotional impact of an account I might have read in a newspaper. For whatever reason, seeing Mindy's image changed that. I studied the college photo with a morbid sense of fascination, coupled with a profoundly sad sense of loss—not for me, but for Jenna. Why did this beautiful person who had so much going for her end up brutally murdered, buried in an anonymous shallow grave? There was so much I didn't know, so much I didn't understand.

I spent the remainder of the afternoon sifting through the files, beginning with the oldest police reports responding to an employee—Mindy—who didn't show up for work and couldn't be reached on her cell, to the eventual conclusion that the case had turned cold, and to its resurrection after the random discovery of human remains in Bulloch County. Shortly before five in the afternoon, Pete Marsh dropped by to see how things were going. "Making any progress?" he asked.

"I feel a little like a guy who has gotten lost in a swamp. There is so much information, so much data to pick through. Pretty daunting task," I replied.

"Welcome to the wonderful world of homicide investigations. Most are pretty straight forward; some guy gets drunk and shoots his buddy on a Saturday night in the presence of a dozen witnesses. But then there are the really tough, nearly impossible cases, like this one. Several law enforcement agencies—the GBI, Bulloch County, the guys here in Savannah—

have had a go at it and it seems we're still pretty close to square one. I've got you down to spend tomorrow continuing to review what's in these boxes, and then the next morning I asked my retired friend, Jack Garrett, to come by and see if he can be of help. He's an easy-going guy, but one of the sharpest people I've ever met when it comes to cracking tough cases. I think you'll like him."

I was back at police headquarters the next day before nine, and except for a brief lunch and a couple of coffee breaks, I spent the entire day in the windowless room, attempting to systematically sort through the file boxes. It was impossible for me to read everything in detail, so I focused on periodic summary reports, interviews with people who knew Mindy or had worked with her at the club, and what little physical evidence that had been collected. It appeared that the Savannah cops, with some assistance from the GBI, had initially pursued the case with decreasing intensity over about a year, then more or less giving up for lack of further leads. With the discovery and identification of her remains, the case was reopened, generating a flurry of paperwork covering more interviews, plus reports and documents from the crime lab and DNA analysis. With the unknown victim now identified, the two sets of files were merged, but the case was no closer to being solved than it was when Mindy was first reported missing.

By four-thirty my eyes had begun to glaze over, so I carefully placed everything back in its proper place in the files, let the record librarian know I was leaving, and headed home for the evening. I called Jenna to let her know how the day had gone. She seemed somewhat encouraged, but at the same time disappointed that I could not report some new revelation. I told her I would keep trying.

On my third day at police headquarters, I arrived just before nine to find the door to the small room slightly open, the six boxes stacked neatly on a cart, and a lean, suntanned man sitting at the table. He smiled and rose as I entered. "You must be John O'Toole," he said, extending his hand. "I'm Jack Garrett." I was a bit surprised. I had expected to see a grizzled old cop, somewhat overweight and far beyond his prime. Instead, Garrett's appearance was that of a wiry marathon runner, with piercing brown eyes and close-cropped gray hair. "Pete Marsh speaks well of you. Said you were a fine fellow who'd been through a lot."

"Pete's been a great help with this, getting permission for me to be here and…."

"For this case, the more eyes the better," Garrett interrupted. "Sit down," he continued, taking charge. "Let's get to know one another, and then I'll try to help you get started. If you intend to try to figure out this case, you've picked a tough row to hoe."

"I know…," I said. For the next few minutes we talked, getting acquainted, asking about each other's backgrounds, and why I wanted to get involved.

"So, your girlfriend was Mindy's friend, and she was the one who sorta pushed you into this?" Garrett asked.

"More or less. As long as I've known her, she's always been a rock of stability—someone I could count on to be there if things got rough, but this has been different. I've never seen this side of her."

"Pete Marsh said you were thinking about getting married." Garret smiled.

"Yeah, the idea has been rolling around in my brain. But it seems that's not going anywhere until this Mindy thing comes to some kind of resolution."

"You know the chances of you finding something new, of solving the case, or even moving it in one direction or another are somewhere between slim and nil?"

"I know, but Jenna has said more or less that if there's nothing more to be learned, no greater chance of finding Mindy's killer, she will be satisfied that we tried. Then maybe we can move ahead. That's what I want."

"Let's get started then," Garrett said, sliding his chair closer to the table. "The one thing you have to know, to remember, to respect, is the fact that the folks who have worked on this case for years have—for most of them, anyway—tried their best to find this girl's killer. That's a given. So, if you think about it, that's likely to mean one of two things. First, they didn't discover something, maybe a link to the murderer, or second, they came across it and didn't realize what they had. Most murders are not planned. They just happen, maybe in the course of a robbery, or a dispute that got out of hand, or to eliminate a witness, or so on. That alone might explain why someone tried so hard to hide Mindy's body. We don't know where the murder took place, so we don't have a crime scene and all the clues that it might yield. The main 'evidence'—if I can use that word—in this case are the interviews done with her friends, family, coworkers, and the like. You've got to be grateful to those who tried, but approach this with a high degree of suspicion that something was missed. You cannot think like a cop. You may want to reinterview some folks, ask the same questions that were asked in the original investigation and see if any answers have changed. Talk to her friends again, and to anyone else who might know something. In short, in a failed investigation like this, you don't want to take anything for granted.

"And if you get on to something, don't try to go it on your own. It's best to call in the cavalry. Pete or any detective in the Homicide Division will drop what they're doing in a minute to assist you. One really important thing you have to remember is that you are now acting as an agent of the State of Georgia. That's who would bring formal charges against a killer. In that role, there are a lot of things you could say or do that would give a good defense attorney reason to get the case thrown out. Pete said you went to law school. You should know the routine—Fourth Amendment search violations, Fourteenth Amendment due process stuff. It's easy to make a slip up that lets a killer walk free."

"I've got to be careful, I know," I said, letting his words sink in. "I almost don't know where to begin...."

"No doubt," Garrett replied. "And there is so much data that has been gathered over the years since the murder that it's easy to feel like you don't know where to start. Everyone's different of course, but let me make a suggestion that used to work for me." He stood up and stepped over to the whiteboard, picked up a dry marker and wrote a series of Roman numerals on the surface: I, II, III, IV, etc. "Imagine that this murder is a stage play, a saga, a movie, or what have you. It has characters—the only one we know for certain now is the victim, Mindy—and it has conflict. It has a beginning, a middle and an end. It starts with something, maybe an event, a conversation—I don't know what—but that something begins the chain of events that lead to Mindy's murder. And in the end, something led her killer to try to hide his or her crime. What you would be hoping for is the ability to write that last scene, the one where the cops rush in to collar the suspect and take him—or her—away. I know this sounds kinda hokey, but it's worked for me on several tough cases."

"That easy, eh?" I said, smiling.

"Yep," Garrett replied as he leaned back in his chair, folded his arms over his chest and grinned.

CHAPTER 17

Jack Garrett and I spent the next couple of hours simply talking, covering in a freeform way his philosophy of crime investigation, of discerning what might be important as opposed to what was likely not to be. The more I heard, the more respect I had for the man. He was obviously quite intelligent and seemed to miss the challenges and thrills of police work even while enjoying his retirement. His hobby of gardening had turned into a full-time job of raising flowers in greenhouses and selling them across the southeastern states. "Keeps me occupied," he explained. "My wife enjoys working with me, and we earn a pretty good income to boot." Pete Marsh joined us for lunch, after which I resumed my work on the boxes of files in the windowless room. Jack left me with his contact information and encouragement to call if I had a question or needed his assistance.

By the end of the day, I had begun a list of questions that I thought deserved the most focus. I'd scribbled notes on a legal pad during my morning conversation with Jack. Now, as I searched for some structure to hang my search onto, I ran my finger down the list, trying to decipher what I'd written only hours before. My finger stopped at "MMO," or—as I recalled—motive, means and opportunity, according to Jack the three essentials in solving any homicide. One of the three—means by which Mindy died—was known. She was beaten and strangled. But why? What was the motive? And where and under what circumstances was she killed? What situation led her murderer to commit the crime? Was it planned, or something that happened in the heat of the moment?

I'd drawn two stars next to the notation of "friends and family." There were a lot of statistics available on the relationship between victims and their assailants Jack had noted, but these meant little or nothing in trying to solve a homicide. "The numbers say a murder victim is more likely to die at the hands of a stranger than a friend or member of the family," he explained, "but the numbers are all over the place and not really helpful. And you've got to remember, statistics don't apply in individual cases. Everyone is a suspect until proven otherwise." I had no idea about any other friends or relationships Mindy might have had, especially individuals who were not interviewed by the police, or who refused to talk. I made a mental note to follow up on this.

After nearly an hour I'd made little progress, filling in only about a dozen lines of notes. Just at that moment, there was a knock on the door followed by the record librarian wheeling in another cart topped by two more bankers boxes. "Here are a few more records for you, Mr. O'Toole," she said with all the sweet pleasantness of a dental assistant informing me that the dentist would be in to start my root canal shortly. "These are the documents and interviews relating to the memorial service for the Davis murder victim a few weeks ago. There are photos taken by our surveillance guys and follow up reports on some interviews they did. I believe I saw your photo in there. They didn't interview you, did they?" I wondered if she was being sarcastic.

"Oh, great," I said, feigning joy at having more records dumped on top of those I still had not yet reviewed. "I'll get right on them."

"Well, they'll all be filed and stored under the same case number, so just keep them together." I promised that I would. She gave a pleasant nod and left, quietly closing the door.

I stared at the eight bankers boxes now balanced on top of the cart, then glanced at my watch. It was nearly four-thirty, and I was ready to call it a day. Jenna would be getting off work shortly; I decided to call her to see if she'd let me take her out to dinner somewhere in Claxton.

"That's great," she said, sounding happy to have the chance to see me. "I'll drop Robert at my parents and we can try out that new barbeque place that just opened last month." I said I'd be there by six-thirty.

The restaurant was busy, but mostly with diners ordering takeout. We found a quiet booth tucked away in a corner so we could talk. I explained to Jenna that there appeared to be very little hard evidence that might provide clues to Mindy's going missing. Most of the records of the initial investigation consisted of interviews and police reports, and about all that could be learned from the crime lab examination of her remains was her identity based on DNA, and that she appeared to have died a violent death. The GBI had initially tried to track her cell phone signal, but found nothing. In fact, more than twenty-four hours passed between the time Mindy was last seen, and when she was reported as missing. Even then, the police did not begin a serious investigation until her whereabouts were unknown for more than forty-eight hours. "So much of what is known of the circumstances of events comes from interviews. And another point made by investigators after the discovery in Bulloch County was the fact that no one has any real idea as to when she was killed. She could have been alive for two weeks, a month, or more after she disappeared...."

"Was she kidnapped and held prisoner or something like that?" Jenna asked, her voice trembling.

"There is no way to know. Two big questions have to be answered: Why was Mindy murdered, and who was her killer?" Jenna stared at her plate, silent. "This—her death—happened years ago, and about the only solid information came from those interviewed." I paused, then added, "And that did not appear to be helpful."

"Can we go home now?" Jenna asked softly. "I think I'm going to be sick." I dropped her off at her apartment. She didn't invite me in, and mentioned as we drove that she'd ask her parents to let her son spend the night at their house. I spent the hour's drive back to Savannah wondering if things would ever be the same.

The following morning I was back at police headquarters by nine, dealing with the conflicting emotions of following through with my promise to Jenna to try to find out more about Mindy's death, or alternatively, walking away from the whole thing and getting on with my life, presumably without her. For the moment at least, I would carry on as planned, but keep all of my options open.

My ruminations overnight had left me with the conclusion that I needed to focus on the interviews made initially and the few more made after the confirmation of Mindy's death. I had not yet looked at the two boxes with the most recent data and photos gathered at the memorial service, so I needed to start with that. This time, the files were not as tightly packed, allowing me to estimate that I could finish reviewing them before the end of the day.

It appeared that the surveillance team from the Savannah police had managed to photograph and identify each of the ninety-four people who attended the service. With great meticulousness, someone had prepared a list, sorting the attendees into groups. Twenty-one were considered "Relatives," including Mindy's mother and brother, and eleven cousins who were accompanied by eight spouses. Thirty-four were listed as "Friends," but this included several spouses. Six had worked with her at the club; eighteen were classmates from high school or college. The remaining fifteen were listed as "Miscellaneous" and included four "Club Patrons," two "Former Teachers," and nine "Unknown Connection." The list of the attendees assigned a number to each name, which corresponded to numbered photographs printed on separate sheets. Jenna and I were grouped with "Friends" and assigned numbers seventy-two and seventy-three, respectively.

Curious, I flipped through the photos looking for the image of the man Jenna had slapped. He was Carlton Lee, one of the four "Club Patrons." A notation next to his name stated that he had been interviewed about two weeks after the service. Interview notes were filed in a separate folder under his name. I felt a sudden eagerness to drop everything and find out exactly what he had to say, but instead decided I would proceed in an orderly fashion and complete my general overview first.

Over the course of the days I spent reviewing the case files, and based on my conversations with Jack Garrett, it had become evident to me that if new information was to be discovered, it would not be through a search for more hard evidence or physical clues, but rather gleaned from interviews with persons who were in some way close to Mindy, or the situation in general. There were no "crime scenes" per se, and it appeared that investigators had done a very adequate job of searching Mindy's apartment, her locker at the club, her computer and emails, the records of her phone calls and texts and so on. It was a long shot, of course, but someone on the list of those interviewed during both investigations must have known more than they revealed. Perhaps it was something trivial to them, a fact, an event, a relationship that seemed to have no bearing on the case. As Jack pointed out, dozens of well-qualified people had tried their best to find the magic thread that would unravel the secret. The chances of my succeeding after their failure were small, but I was determined to try.

CHAPTER 18

Having decided the initial direction my search would take, I settled down and began making a list of whom to contact. I had little doubt that a number of those interviewed in the days after Mindy's disappearance would not be available. It had been several years, of course, and I suspected that many, perhaps most, would say that they had nothing to add to their initial statements. Others though, Mindy's family, people who continued to work at the club, some close friends, perhaps teachers or instructors who had known her in high school or college, might be worthwhile candidates to talk with. And certainly, anyone who had been initially contacted by investigators, and later attended the memorial service needed to be gently reinterviewed. As the person making the inquiry, I needed to present a positive image, the close friend of a close friend of Mindy trying to help bring some closure—there was that dreadful word again—to those affected by her death.

I decided to start with the low-hanging fruit. Digging through the initial six boxes of investigation files, I found a list of persons interviewed in the weeks and months following Mindy's disappearance. Comparing this with the list of the ninety-four people who attended the memorial service, I found an overlap of a dozen names, persons who had been questioned twice by investigators. These included the obvious candidates, Mindy's mother and brother, several club coworkers and patrons, two college instructors, and two females who had known her during college and graduate school at Georgia Southern University. I noticed Carlton Lee, the man Jenna slapped, was on the list, but other than the mother and brother, I didn't recognize any of the names. To get started, attempting to meet with some or all of the twelve would be enough to see if the process was worthwhile before delving deeper with more interviews. I briefly considered sharing the list with Jenna, perhaps asking her advice or perspective, but thought better of it. It would only serve to upset her. I decided I would tell her that I was reinterviewing some people, but not share names unless she specifically asked.

I looked over the list of names I'd written on a legal pad, wondering where to start. After a few minutes of thought decided I would begin with what was likely to be the most informative interview, and also probably the most difficult, Mindy's mother. She had met me at the memorial service with Jenna, so I could assume she knew I was a friend. But my acting in the role of investigator was a different matter, in her case at least. I was certain she and Pete Marsh had met during the course of the investigations. I called and asked if he would contact her, explain what I was doing, and provide a bit of introduction. He said he would. Twenty minutes later he called back to say he'd taken care of things. He gave me Mrs. Davis's number and suggested I call her while things were still fresh in her mind. I glanced at my watch, waited fifteen minutes and called.

The phone rang twice, followed by a click and a meek "Hello."

"Mrs. Davis," I began, "This is John O'Toole. I believe you just spoke with Pete Marsh. I'm working with the Savannah police to follow up on some…."

"Yes, I know, Mr. O'Toole. Mr. Marsh said you'd be calling, and gave you his endorsement. He's a fine man, and I appreciate—no, we all appreciate—what you're doing." She hesitated briefly. "So you'd like to interview me again about all that happened, is that right?"

"Yes, ma'am, if it's convenient. I know you've been through a lot over these past years. I don't want to intrude, but I'm trying to help out by taking a fresh look at things—for you, for Mindy, and for Jenna."

"Mr. Marsh said you and Jenna were thinking about getting married."

"The thought is there, but we've not made any definite plans as yet," I replied, wishing Pete would limit his comments to the fact that Jenna and I were just friends at this point.

"Well, that's fine. We loved Jenna when she and Mindy were in school.... When would you like to talk? I presume you want to come here to Vidalia?" I told her any time that was convenient with her. "How about tomorrow morning then, about ten o'clock? Will that work?" I said that would be fine. She gave me her address and told me to just park in front of the house.

I looked up the Davises' address and direction there on Google Maps. It was about ninety miles, and essentially all expressway and four-lane if I took I-16 and cut off on US Hwy 1. I decided to leave at 8:00 a.m., and settled down in an armchair to work up a group of questions. The material I'd been given had summaries of both Mrs. Davis's initial and subsequent interviews. At first glance, it appeared that the information she provided, either on her own or in response to the investigator's questions, was of little help. I tried to think of other routes of inquiry, but decided in the end to simply take a blank legal pad and see where the conversation would lead.

Vidalia, like many smaller towns in south Georgia, grew up around a railroad junction. With a population of about ten thousand that has been stable for decades, it is best known for the area's production of its eponymic onions which hold the dubious honor of being the official vegetable of the state of Georgia. The Davis residence was located in the northern part of the city in a neighborhood of large homes set on even larger lots. The initial impression was one of discreet wealth. I parked in the circular driveway and rang the doorbell. The maid opened the door and ushered me into a formal parlor overlooking the front expanse of lawn. "Miz Davis be comin'," she said and motioned for me to make myself comfortable.

I surveyed the room. A large fireplace was flanked by bookshelves with an assortment of high-brow books, including a pristine multi-volume set of Will and Ariel Durant's *The Story of Civilization.* Several photos in polished silver frames appeared to be images of the Davis family. I recognized Mindy from the photo I'd seen, and her brother Peter from the memorial service. A fresh spray of flowers sprang from a cut crystal vase.

Mrs. Davis appeared shortly, smiling and thanking me for my interest in her daughter's case. "To be honest, Mr. O'Toole, I had given up hope on ever seeing justice for Mindy's killer. I so appreciate your efforts. Perhaps you'll succeed where others have failed." Although I had met her briefly at the memorial service, this time I studied her in more detail. She appeared to be in her late sixties, but I suspected her actual age to be younger. The loss of her husband and daughter had taken its toll. For the next ten minutes or so we exchanged pleasantries, seeming to gauge each other's motivations and goals. Mrs. Davis clearly wanted to know who killed her daughter and why. She acknowledged my relationship with Jenna and did not seem suspicious of my interest in the case.

Getting down to a discussion of the events surrounding Mindy's disappearance, I reviewed with her the things she had mentioned to previous interviewers. She said that she had been as honest and forthright as she knew she had to be, but in addition to losing her daughter, "having to discuss Mindy's lifestyle," as she termed it, was humiliating and embarrassing. "Let me explain something, Mr. O'Toole. I didn't discuss this with the police, but at this point I might as well talk about it with you, at least." She paused, glanced around the room and began. "You look at this fine house that sits in this neighborhood of fine homes. You know my late husband was a doctor, and I'd guess most people would think we were wealthy. Well, we were, in a sort of way at one time. But not now.

"You were at the memorial service. That church is where my husband and I were married, and the graveyard there is where he's buried. But the truth is different." She spoke with intensity, her eyes gleaming. "We were both born and raised within two miles of that church. Both of our parents were sharecroppers who saved enough to buy small farms, just enough to feed and clothe their children, but not much else. I was raised poor, Mr. O'Toole, and so was Daniel, my husband. He was my first and my only boyfriend—ever since the eighth grade. And I'm pretty sure I was his only girlfriend. When we were young we both swore that we'd get off the farm, get married and make a better life for our children than we had. So we did. We were both nineteen when we tied the knot. We agreed—in advance—that I would work and Dan would go to college and then try to go to medical school. For years I worked right here in Vidalia at a sewing factory, doing common labor for very little pay, and Dan got a scholarship and went to Georgia Southern. He worked weeknights in a convenience store to help support us. About the only time I got to see him was on the weekends. He did well—straight A's; got a full scholarship to the Medical College of Georgia. And it was only when we were both pushing thirty years of age that we could start a family and offer them more than we'd had coming up.

"We both inherited a little land from our parents. I sold mine to make a down payment on this house. We kept Dan's land—it isn't much, just eighty acres or so with an old farmhouse—but it reminded us of where we came from. It was supposed to go to both Mindy and Peter, but with Mindy gone it belongs to Peter now. We used to go there for Thanksgiving and Christmas, but I haven't been there since Mindy went missing. I just stay here in this golden prison thinking how miserable I am. My son, like his daddy, is a doctor now. He's moved away. Dan died—you knew that, I guess—and I have nothing, no one to live for." Fighting back tears, Mrs. Davis stared out the window as she tried to regain her composure.

"But tell me more about Mindy," I said, trying to get the conversation back on track.

"I was getting to that," Mrs. Davis said, clenching her jaws. "Dan died suddenly and unexpectedly of a stroke. There was some insurance money that helped out for a while, but pretty soon that was running out. And Peter, her older brother, was in medical school and residency and was making barely enough to live on. So, Mindy took this job at a restaurant—that's what she called it, a restaurant—there in Savannah and was making good money, enough to send a nice check every week or two to help out here. Otherwise, the bank would have foreclosed on this house and I'd be on the street. Peter's been helping support me since Mindy's been gone. I get by, but not much more." As she spoke, I wondered how she could afford to pay the maid.

CHAPTER 19

"You see, Mr. O'Toole, my husband and I struggled for so long to pull ourselves up in the world, sacrificing our younger years so Peter and Mindy wouldn't have to grow up like we did, the barefoot kids of sharecroppers. And we made it, and then it all came crashing down when Dan died. Oh, Peter's done well for sure, but Mindy—poor Mindy—despite all the fine education we paid for turned into a…, a…." She stopped, choked up, then, "…a stripper, a drug user, and—I suspect—a common whore." She paused again; I said nothing. "It's horrible in so many ways." Once more Mrs. Davis was silent, momentarily staring out the window again before turning to me and continuing with a note of sarcasm and irony, "And now she's dead, and yet here I am, living my dreams."

I was confused. On one hand, Mindy's choices help support her mother's lifestyle, yet Mrs. Davis seemed to bitterly resent them. Certainly she was sorrowful at the loss of her daughter, but I also sensed a component of betrayal and anger directed at her. Jenna had never mentioned Mindy helping support her mother, but she may not have known. I decided to ask her about it the next time we talked. I couldn't quite figure out where Mrs. Davis was coming from. Even after her husband's and daughter's deaths, she continued to live in the big, lonely house. And she kept a maid, in addition to having to pay maintenance, property taxes and the like. It had to be expensive, and she seemed to make it clear that she had no income except for the support she received from her son. Why didn't she face reality and downsize?

We talked for another half-hour, but our conversation produced no further revelations. Mrs. Davis invited me to stay for lunch. I politely declined, saying I needed to get back to Savannah and my obligations there. Driving home, I wondered how I should summarize my visit. I wasn't at all sure that it had been productive. The words anger, resentment, humiliation, and embarrassment caused by and directed at Mindy came to mind, even more so than sorrow and a sense of loss.

Back in Savannah, I checked in at the gallery to see if I was needed. Jessica assured me all was well, with several large sales since I'd been "distracted." I holed up in my office long enough to review the mail and sign checks for bills due, then retreated to my apartment above the carriage house to think. I worried that the two hours I spent meeting with Mindy's mother had been a waste of time. She was clearly dealing with her own demons surrounding her daughter's death, and our conversation added little to my understanding of the case. I had earlier considered next trying to interview Mindy's cardiologist brother, Dr. Peter Davis. He practiced in Savannah, and according to the case file lived on Skidaway Island, an enclave of upscale homes nearer the coast. Setting up a time to talk would be a simple matter, assuming he was willing to meet with me. After my less than ideal interaction with his mother, however, I decided to go in a different direction, choosing another name from the list.

Consulting the roster of those who had been interviewed after Mindy's disappearance and who'd also attended the memorial service, I elected trying to speak next with one of the two people listed as Mindy's college instructors. The first, a Camilla DuBose, had been described as a former Assistant Professor of Art History at Georgia Southern. The notes I'd made said she was now living in Atlanta and apparently teaching at Georgia State. The second was Pablo Martinez, PhD, whose given address was Brooklet, Georgia, less than an hour's drive from Savannah. No phone number was listed. That option seemed most convenient. A google search yielded a photo—middle-aged, brown hair with Van Dyke moustache and beard suggesting a painterly look, or so I assumed. A brief online bio said he was an expert on art of the Middle Ages, an artist who had lectured at several universities, and was available for portraiture or other commissions. I wasn't precisely sure what that meant, but presumably he supported himself through the sale of his paintings. A contact number was listed. Even though he had attended the memorial service, I couldn't recall seeing him. Perhaps he had shaved his facial hair. I thought it best to check with Jenna before I decided which of the two instructors to interview first.

As it was nearly 6:00 p.m., I called Jenna on her cell, thinking she'd probably be at home. She answered promptly, sounding happy to hear my voice. "How did the visit with Mindy's mother go today?" she asked.

"Fairly good, I guess. I can't say that I learned a lot, other than Mrs. Davis appears to be terribly bitter about things. Even though her only daughter is gone, she seemed more angry than sorrowful."

"Hmm," Jenna said, evidently processing the information. "I guess I'm not surprised. I'm sure she loved Mindy, and was loved in return, but she deeply resented Mindy working at the club. I remember some terrible screaming matches over the phone several times when I was staying over at her place. Afterwards Mindy would end up crying for the longest. And the sad part is that she sent a big chunk of what she made back to her mother, trying to help out since her father died. The Davises always came across—to me, anyway—as upscale people, and Mindy was an embarrassment, a daughter gone bad, someone they were privately ashamed of. Of course, they covered all that up. I'd never have known in a million years if we hadn't been close friends."

"Did she ever talk to you about it? Like how she felt, or things like that?"

"Not really. Sometimes I'd try to help, but her response was always 'A girl's gotta do what a girl's gotta do,' whatever that means. So she worked at the club and sent home a check about every week, I think."

"Okay," I said, temporarily dismissing the subject. "One of the reasons I called was to get your thoughts on whom I should interview next. I'm starting with the small group of people who were interviewed when Mindy first went missing, and who later came to the memorial service. I was going to try to talk next to Mindy's brother, but I'll wait. I have the names of two instructors—teachers, professors or whatever. One is Camilla DuBose. She lives in Atlanta now, and that's a long way off. The other, a PhD guy named Pablo Martinez, lives in...."

"No! Not Pablo. I didn't see him at the service. He's...."

"I googled him and found a photo. I don't recall seeing him either. He had a beard, very distinctive, but I think he may have shaved...."

"You said you googled him?" Jenna broke in.

"Yeah."

"What else did you find?"

"What do you mean?"

"Did you know he's been banned from the Georgia Southern campus and probably blacklisted from teaching in a public institution just about anywhere?" Jenna seemed upset at the mention of Martinez's name.

"No, but I was just looking for contact information. I clicked on the top result, and it had what I was looking for. I didn't look at the rest of the hits."

"He's a pervert, John. A sleezy, nasty middle-aged man who probably took up teaching so he could hit on college girls. I think, but I'm not really sure, that he and Mindy had something going at one time. He was the one who turned her on to the painting, *The Garden of Earthly Delights*. Oh, yeah, I'm sure he's qualified and has a PhD and is a good painter and knows about art, but...," she hesitated, "...he tries to seduce innocent freshman and sophomores with his BS about the mystery and beauty and transcendental nature of art when his real goal is to get in their pants. He even came after me once, but I saw him for what he was." Jenna stopped, now breathing rapidly.

"But what were you saying about this guy and Mindy?"

"On a certain level they seemed to get along," Jenna explained. "I hate to say it because she was a good friend, but Mindy's moral compass was a little looser than most people's. Martinez was always willing to 'help out,' as he liked to say, usually with a couple of twenties, or maybe fifty bucks, or more. Mindy milked him like the cash cow that he was and then turned around and sent it back to her mother."

"So, he was at Georgia Southern as a professor?"

"Adjunct professor—teaching a course in Art of the Middle Ages. This is when Mindy and I were in our Junior and Senior years."

"He left?"

"He wasn't full time. Just there to fill out the Art Department faculty for that course. And he didn't leave—he was kicked off campus after one, and then another, and then a third and more girls accused him of sexual harassment. It all got covered up mostly. But later I remember reading somewhere that he was charged with the same sort of thing that ended up in court. You can probably find it online if you look."

"Not a nice guy, eh?"

"Terrible," Jenna said.

"Think he would hurt Mindy?"

"I don't have any idea, but I hope you'll interview him. I wouldn't rule it out."

CHAPTER 20

After considering my options, I decided to try to interview Martinez next. The investigators who had worked on Mindy's case had, on numerous places in the record, termed it a "sex crime." I had earlier asked Jack Garrett about that designation as it appeared to me that there was no clear evidence that sex had anything to do with it. "It's just an assumption," he said, "but in this case quite possibly a valid one. We know Mindy was a stripper who sometimes went on 'dates' with various men. The exam of her remains strongly suggested she was naked when her body was buried. And there was violence—she was beaten and strangled. It fits a common—and unfortunately often repeated—pattern. Sexual assault, 'rape' if you will, is a crime of violence. And the victims are sometimes murdered." I realized I needed to be well-prepared before I tried to interview the former professor.

My first task was to review his two prior interviews. Back at police headquarters, I pulled the files and set out to study them—noting that on both occasions his interviewers did not know of his fondness for sexually harassing his female students. The first, done about four weeks after Mindy's disappearance, was revealing. Martinez readily admitted to having an intermittent "relationship" with her that spanned several years from her college days through graduate school. He said he had visited the club where she worked maybe half a dozen times, but stated "it wasn't really my style" and that he "felt out of place there." At the interview following the memorial service, Martinez explained that Mindy was one of the most memorable students he'd ever taught, and attended simply because he wanted to show his respect to her family and friends. The interviewer made a note that his name was not listed on the Georgia Bureau of Investigation's online Sex Offender Registry. All considered, neither interview was helpful. Following Jenna's suggestion, I decided to dig deeper online.

Again, I entered "Pablo Martinez" in the search bar on my computer, and came up with what I'd found earlier, photos and reviews of his paintings, the fact that he had taught at Georgia Southern and so on. But then I discovered that "Pablo Martinez" was in fact not the man's name, but instead a "*nom de brosse*," as one website account described it. It seemed that while "Martinez's" PhD and his skill as an artist were quite legitimate, his real name was George Earnest Martin. He had explained to one interviewer that the "Spanishy" pseudonym promoted his exotic image as an artist, citing as justification that the real name of "Dr. Dre," the rapper, was Andre Romelle Young. It made no sense to me at all. And I found that his true name had been mentioned on at least three occasions associated with sexual harassment civil lawsuits. The guy was beginning to look like a nut case, or at the very least, weird. I could only imagine how my interview with him would go, assuming he would agree to meet with me.

Uncertain of the outcome, I dialed Martin's number. He answered promptly; I introduced myself and explained why I was calling. After a bit of back and forth, and assurance I was working with the Savannah police, he agreed to see me, asking, "Will, say, 3:00 p.m. Sunday afternoon work for you?" I said it would. He gave me directions to his house—"A little out of town with a long driveway; you can't see it from the road"—and didn't sound the least bit concerned about being interviewed for the third time in an active murder investigation.

On Sunday I headed for Brooklet. It was a lovely, blue-sky fall day, so I took the back roads, long stretches of asphalt running through miles of fields and forests interspersed with the occasional home or farm. I arrived about fifteen minutes early, stopping in the parking lot of the local IGA Food Store to get my bearings. I was to head north about three and a half miles, searching for a bright yellow mailbox next to a gravel drive on the left side of the road. The drive followed the edge of a large field of peanuts, then disappeared into a pine grove half a mile in the distance. After another several hundred yards, the road ended at a grand old wooden farmhouse, with a sweeping front porch and peeling white paint. To the rear of the house I could see a large windowless metal building, no doubt a century or more younger than its wooden neighbor. A clean-shaven, middle-aged man whom I presumed was George Earnest Martin, a.k.a. Pablo Martinez, was sitting in one of the half-dozen rocking chairs lined up on the farmhouse porch. He stood up and walked down the front steps to greet me. "Mr. O'Toole! Welcome to my home! I am so pleased to meet you, and so happy that someone is finally following up on the horrible things that happened to our poor Mindy."

"Yes, I agreed to look over what had been done, hoping to get some new leads. That's why I was talking with a few people who had originally discussed the case with the investigators," I said.

"I did. Twice." Martin grinned.

"I know," I replied and he momentarily frowned.

"Let's go out to my studio. I have a nice shady spot to sit and talk," he said, motioning me to follow him around the house to the building in the rear. On the far side under a large overhanging porch, a collection of cushioned chairs looked out toward the pine forest in the distance. "Can I get you something to drink?" Martin asked. "Water, soft drinks, beer, or perhaps something stronger…?"

"No, thank you, I'm fine." He was being obsequiously friendly.

We sat down and chatted for a few moments. "Do you live here alone?" I asked.

"Oh, yes. I'm an artist, and inspiration is something that can arise suddenly and last for days without letup. I make most of my living creating works of art—custom orders, commissions, mostly. Creativity is a deep ineffable sensation that guides my brushstrokes, an unutterable, inexpressible feeling honed through years of training, something that guides our limbic urges to the pinnacle of human joy and ecstasy…."

I had to stop him before his spiel got out of hand. Smiling, I interrupted him with, "I understand that Martinez is your professional name, but your given name is George Martin, is that correct?"

Martin stopped suddenly, looking at me like I had just slapped him. "Yeah," he said, his voice now with a different tone. "It's a marketing thing, really. You know Picasso's first name was Pablo. It helps. I can even do a Spanish accent if I have to."

"No, that's okay, but thanks. Let's talk about Mindy, and what you remember that might be important."

His artist persona and pretense now dropped, we talked at length about Mindy, and his relationship with her over several years. "We were involved, yeah. I can't deny that. I think she liked me and probably enjoyed my company, but I gave her money. I inherited pretty well, Mr. O'Toole, and that allows me to say I make a living as a painter. But in truth, most of it comes from trust funds set up by my grandfather. And that's probably the biggest secret I have. I want people to think I make it from the sale of my art."

"How did Mindy feel about that? I mean she was close to twenty and you were...?

"A lot older." Martin finished my sentence. "I know, but hell, life is short, so why not?" I silently noted that he didn't answer my question.

"And there were some problems with allegations of sexual harassment, I understand?"

Martin sat up and looked surprised. "How did you find out about that?"

"Google."

"Oh, so it's online now. Shit! We settled those issues and the court agreed to seal the records." Martin clenched his teeth.

"I'm sure they did as far as the details go, but the reason for the filing of any civil suit can be found with minimal digging. Everybody's going digital, and most of that stuff is public record now."

"Oh," he said again. "You want to see my studio?" Apparently the interview was over.

I smiled and said, "I'd love to, thanks."

I followed Martin through a door connecting the porch to the main section of the building. We entered a large windowless high-ceilinged room with a series of easels supporting moderate-sized canvases in varying degrees of completion. "I guess I'm a little peculiar," he admitted. "I'm usually working on more than one canvas at any time. I wasn't kidding about the inspiration part, so when I hit a creative wall on one, I move to the next."

"Why no windows? I thought artists loved natural light."

"Back when, yeah. But with today's LEDs I can create any mood I want from sunrise to the post-sunset blue hour. Works better for me."

"This is a huge building," I said. "What's in the rest of it?"

"Some is storage. And a big part of it is a project I've been working on for years—a diorama."

"Diorama?" The word was familiar but for the moment I couldn't place it.

"You know, like the Cyclorama of the Battle of Atlanta. It used to be at Grant Park near where I grew up, but they moved it to the Atlanta History Center several years ago. A diorama is a huge 3-D installation with a painted backdrop and realistic figures depicting something—like a battle, or a scene from mythology or the like. Someone once told me they were the old-time forerunners of IMAX theaters."

"Sounds like a major project. What's yours about?"

Martin paused, seemingly trying to decide if he should tell me more. "Like I said, it's something I've been working on for a long time. A huge project." He paused again, then, "I have a PhD in Art, you know. My thesis was on religious expression in the art of the Late Middle Ages. There are so many works that lend themselves to something beyond the flat expression of color on canvas. It's a work in progress, and while I'm getting there, I've still got a long way to go. Do you really want to see it?"

"Yes, I'd like that very much."

"Will you keep this in confidence? I don't think most people would understand," Martin asked.

"I promise."

"Okay, then." He stepped forward and ushered me into a cavernous space illuminated only by a few nightlights spaced along the walls. "Wait here," he said. "I need to turn on the spotlights." He stepped away and in a moment the room was flooded with brilliant white lights focused on a low platform placed against one wall of the huge room. Images of fantastic beasts mingled with dozens of naked figures in the foreground. Strange structures protruded from a garden-like setting. A flat area in the distance was painted to resemble a pool filled with water, while blue orbs and phallic-like structures loomed in front of the distant horizon.

"It's not completely finished, but how do you like it?" Martin asked.

More than anything else, it was an amazing, strange, wild collage of images and figures. "What is it?" I asked.

"The image of Paradise. A diorama of the central panel of Hieronymus Bosch's *The Garden of Earthly Delights.*"

CHAPTER 21

"This painting, this magnificent work of art, was the subject of my doctoral thesis," Martin said proudly. "Even though Bosch created it more than 500 years ago, the questions it raises about the vibrant and effervescent nature of all art transcend the centuries. Volumes have been written on the interpretation of his graphic symbolism and the occult nature of its meaning." Martin seemed to be drifting back into his obfuscation mode.

"It's really quite impressive," I said, referring to the massive diorama he had created.

"Yes…, and we could stand here for hours as I pointed out individual characters and their allegorical meaning. Look, if you're interested, I had illustrated copies of my thesis printed and bound. I'd be happy to give you one."

"Sure," I said. "I'd appreciate that." Anything to end the conversation.

Martin grinned. "They're in the house. Make yourself comfortable while I go get a copy for you." With that, he disappeared through the door, leaving me in the empty room with its massive painting and its naked figures. I walked toward the construction in order to examine it more closely. The figures in the foreground were realistic and humanoid, but constructed of what appeared to be paper-mache with carefully drawn expressions and facial features. There were other props of sorts, Martin's versions of the strange shapes and objects in the painting. The background, drawn as a colorful landscape with a sense of depth, was a massive canvas. He must have spent hundreds of hours creating it. I had to give him credit; he was amazingly talented as an artist. Reality aside, the two-dimensional images of the painting morphed into life-sized three-dimensional figures. With a bit of imagination, it would easily have been possible to imagine oneself in Bosch's vision of Paradise.

After about ten minutes, Martin reentered the room carrying a hefty volume in his hands. I had expected a typewritten copy of his thesis, but instead he carried a hard-bound, coffee-tabled sized book with a colorful and complicated illustration on the cover. He held it out to me proudly. The first thing I noticed were large illuminated letters, "BDSM," vertically placed and drawn in a Medieval style. "Wow," I said, genuinely impressed. On more closely examining the cover, I realized the letters were part of the title of the thesis, *Bosch's Dilemma: Symbolism and Meaning.*

"I originally had these printed for my family and a few favorite students. But I've discovered they sell well. You can buy a copy on Amazon."

"Oh, let me pay you for this then," I said.

"No, I wouldn't hear of that. It's a gift."

"Thank you. I know I'll enjoy reading it."

"It's kind of weighty, from an artistic and intellectual standpoint," Martin said. "May I sign it for you?"

"Yes, please do."

Walking over to a small table near the door, Martin sat down, took a pen from a drawer, and asked, "Would you like an inscription, or just my signature?"

"Just your signature will be fine, thanks," I replied, noting as he signed that he was left-handed. "I appreciate your giving me the book. You've been very helpful, but there are just a couple of more things I want ask about before I leave. Nothing to do with Mindy or the investigation; just curiosity."

"Oh, okay," Martin said. "Ask away."

"I understand you're not teaching now, but in the past did your students ever come here to your studio? You're just a short ride from the Statesboro campus."

"Oh, yes, frequently. This room, this diorama, I used as a teaching tool. You see, Mr. O'Toole, graphic art is quintessentially a visual medium, but it's also something your brain translates into feelings and emotions. Think of religious art—say Christ on the Cross. A believer would feel sad for His suffering, or grateful for salvation, and so on. Personally, I'm not into all that, but you get the idea. The symbolism of *The Garden of Earthly Delights* has been interpreted and reinterpreted for half a millennium, and almost every scholar sees something different. I designed this construction to represent the middle panel of the triptych, the largest part of the painting. It's not the Garden of Eden on one side, or of Hell on the other, but rather an image of Paradise before the Fall of Man that took place when Adam and Eve ate the forbidden fruit from the Tree of Knowledge of Good and Evil. Look at the figures," Martin said, gesturing, "they are naked. There was no shame, only purity and love..."

"By 'love,' do you mean sex?" I asked.

"Well, that, too, but it was pure."

"So how did you use the diorama as a 'teaching tool'?"

"I encouraged the students to imagine themselves living in Paradise, to pose with the figures, to act out what they thought they would do in Paradise...."

"Okay," I said, having heard enough. I could imagine Martin talking his naïve students into getting naked and prancing about while he supervised. Education and doctoral degree aside, the guy clearly had problems. "One more thing. Did you ever know a girl named Jenna?"

"Mindy's friend? Of course. She was here a number of times. She took several classes I taught."

"Did she ever join in the celebration of Paradise here?"

Martin hesitated before answering, "Well, kinda..., really more yes and no. It was during a workshop, you know, a practicum. The purpose was to imagine what Bosch was thinking when he created this work, to literally put oneself in the picture as represented by the diorama. She was really reluctant to join the other students acting out their roles. She got upset and left. I was forced to give her an 'incomplete' in the class. No credit hours."

"Oh, okay," I said, trying not to visibly react. How had this pervert avoided the Sex Offender Registry? I didn't mention being at Mindy's memorial service. Apparently Martin didn't remember me and had not recognized Jenna. "If you don't mind, I have one final question before I leave. Why did you shave your moustache and beard?"

Martin chuckled, "Well, to be honest, with the various problems that came up...."

"You mean the sexual harassment allegations?" I interrupted.

"Yeah, er..., my photo somehow got in the paper, and I thought maybe it might be best to sort of change my appearance. You do know that I strenuously denied what they were saying, but once these damned lawyers find you've got a little money they attack like a pack of rabid dogs...."

"I see," I said, wishing him well and taking my leave. I had a urgent desire to take a long hot shower to scrub away any lingering traces of my visit.

It was late in the day by the time I got back to Savannah. Being Sunday, the gallery was closed, the noise of traffic minimal and the air cool. I sat outside on the front porch of my apartment overlooking the courtyard, trying to decide if I should tell Jenna that I'd met with Martin, or Dr. Martinez, as she probably knew him. I knew that would upset her, so I elected not to unless she asked me specifically. On the other hand, she might find out anyway and be hurt that I didn't voluntarily tell her. So, I called, opting to try a different tack. "Hey," she said, answering promptly. "How's your Sunday going?"

"Good. Just taking it easy, thinking about all the things I've got to do on this case." I paused a bit and then, trying to sound spontaneous, said, "That reminds me. You remember the prof we spoke about, the Martinez guy?"

"How could I forget?"

"Think I should meet with him? You told me he was hitting on you, and sounded like a lowlife, but still…."

"Oh, yes, for sure," Jenna said confidently. "He's someone I would have put high up on the suspect list if they'd asked me. I never heard of anything violent he did to anyone, but Mindy told me he was a control freak, liked to be in charge, to tell people what to do, or if that didn't work, trick them or coerce them into doing it."

"But you never shared this with the investigators?"

"They didn't ask me. I was mostly in rehab around that time, remember? And for the longest time after that I tried to stay away from the club scene and all the temptations that went with it. I only got back into it once I felt psychologically strong enough."

"Good," I said, and changed the subject.

CHAPTER 22

I wasn't at all sure how productive my first two interviews had been. Yes, I had been surprised at Mrs. Davis's attitude, and confirmed what a number of people already knew or suspected about the lecherous Dr. Martinez, but neither rose to the level of shocking epiphany when it came to the basic questions of the who and why surrounding Mindy's murder. But on the other hand, all this was new to me. I wasn't a Jack Garrett or a Pete Marsh, hardened and cynical after hundreds, perhaps thousands, of similar interviews over the years. I was still learning on the job. I needed to forge ahead.

I feared that speaking with Dr. Davis might be as unproductive as my conversation with his mother, so I decided next to try to interview Carlton Lee. The previous interview reports indicated that he was now fifty-one-years-old, divorced, and worked as a supervisor at a Savannah construction firm. No home address was given, but his cell phone number was listed. He was supposedly a regular patron of the strip club and had remembered Jenna, much to her dismay. I called his cell and got no answer. I gave my name, a brief reason for my call, and asked him to get in touch. He called back less than two minutes after I hung up. A gruff voice on the other end of the line said, "Is this John O'Toole? I hear you want to talk with me."

"Yes, I'm working as an investigator with the Savannah police. We're taking a fresh look at the Mindy Davis murder. I know you've been interviewed twice before, but we wanted to...."

“Look here, Mr. O’Toole. I told those guys I didn’t have nothing to do with Mindy’s killing. Sure, we was friends and all that but....”

“No one thinks you’re a suspect, Mr. Lee,” I said. “It’s just that we’re trying to talk again with folks who knew her, who might know or have remembered some things that didn’t seem important at the time—that sort of thing.”

“Oh,” Lee said. “Just tilling old ground?”

“More or less.”

“Yeah, sure, I’ll meet with you. I cared about Mindy, I really did. I woulda married her if I could, but I was married to someone else at the time and, well..., we can talk about it. When and where do you want to get together?”

“Your call, I’d guess. Somewhere quiet and a bit private so we can talk without interruption.”

“Lemme think...,” Lee said. Then, “How about the A-2-Z Cafeteria out on Abercorn near the mall? They’re an all-you-can-eat place, but around three in the afternoon it’s pretty much empty. I’m off tomorrow if that will work.”

“Sounds good,” I said. “I’ll be there.”

“Okay, but wait—tell me how I’m gonna know it’s you.”

“Remember the memorial service, you saw ‘Candi’ there.”

“Yeah....”

“I was the guy with her. See you tomorrow.” I hung up. In the back of my mind, I worried that Lee might not show up, thinking perhaps that as the person accompanying Jenna—or “Candi” to him—I was somehow upset with him. But we’d just have to see....

The A-2-Z Cafeteria was a well-known spot for those concerned with consuming the maximum number of calories for the lowest cost in a setting essentially devoid of what most dining establishments would term "service." Surprisingly, its dining clientele spanned the economic spectrum from the unwashed homeless, to suburban mothers accompanied by a gaggle of children. I arrived early and grabbed a seat in a booth with a view of the door, telling the waitress I was expecting another person. Lee showed up on the hour, wearing steel-toed boots, blue jeans and a faded gray work shirt with an embroidered patch reading "Carl" above the left pocket. He recognized me immediately and tentatively slid into the seat across from me. "I hope you ain't upset about what I said to Candi. Is she your girlfriend or something?"

I smiled and said, "Not at all. She just needed someone to come to the service with her, and I got volunteered." Lee looked somewhat relieved.

"So y'all two ain't dating or nothing like that?"

"No," I lied. "I've just known her for a while."

Lee visibly relaxed. "So, what can I help you with?"

I explained that I was working as an investigator on Mindy Davis's murder, which had become a cold case. The previous investigations had not produced any firm leads, and we decided to take a fresh look one last time before giving up. I deliberately kept the exact details vague. We told the waitress we were just having coffee and dessert, and began our conversation.

Lee said he'd met Mindy at the club. "I used to not go there all that much. I mean I was married and all, but when that started to come apart I was there a pretty good bit. And I was drinking too much around that time, too. Mindy was good looking, smart and I think she was educated even, or had been to college. She was kinda available for a good time, too, if you know what I mean, but it was real expensive, so I couldn't do a lot of that."

"Did you ever see her outside the club? Like go on dates or something?" I asked.

"Nah, not really. I got a motel room several times, but then we went to her farm three or four times, too."

"What farm?" I hadn't heard of that.

"Up in the northern part of Toombs County, north of Vidalia. It's in the country about an hour's drive from Savannah and eight or ten miles off of I-16. She'd have some people there, 'parties' she called them. Invite a group of girls from the club, have some beer and liquor, invite a bunch of fellas who enjoyed partying—we'd have fun. But it was expensive—I'd end up spending several hundred dollars."

"Tell me more about that. Was there some sort of event space, like maybe for a wedding reception or something like that?"

"Nah, just an old farmhouse way out in the middle of nowhere, furnished like you'd think an old farmhouse would be, three bedrooms I think, a barn, what used to be a cattle lot.... That kind of place. She said it used to belong to her granddaddy and then her papa, but he died and it was hers now." Lee took a break from talking to spoon some banana cream pie into his mouth. This had to be the same "farm" that Mrs. Davis had mentioned, the one that was left to Mindy and her brother Peter.

"So, Mindy just used the farm for parties?"

"Yeah, but she told me one time her brother was getting upset about it—I don't remember the details."

"Let me ask you about who was there, you said she invited people?"

"Well, not just 'people,' but guys that she knew who were regulars at the club. The sort that wouldn't get too drunk or crazy or start a fight or somethin' like that. She wanted to keep things orderly."

"And the girls?" It was a question I didn't want to ask because I was afraid of the answer.

"Yeah, good girls and bad girls. All of 'em worked at the club or had at one time or another. Some of them was pretty easy—you know, flash a hundred and you're off to the woodshed, or bedroom, or whatever. And not all the guys wanted that. Some of 'em just wanted to talk, or be listened to, or that kind of stuff. You know how it is when you're married—the wife nagging, never paying any attention to things that bother you. All of the girls was good listeners, I know that much, 'cause along that time things were going bad at my house...." Lee stopped in mid-sentence. "You don't want to hear that though, do you?"

"I'm interested in anything you have to say. You never know what might be important," I said.

"Well, that's pretty much all I know about the farm. I do know Mindy made good money. She told me one time that she was sending it to her ma. Maybe that was true, dunno. Maybe she was just looking to squeeze a little more cash out of me."

Nearly biting my tongue, I asked, "Did you ever see Candi there?"

"Sometimes. She wasn't a regular to be sure. I think she had a little kid at home, and she never was into big-time partying like a lot of the other girls." Lee flashed a broad grin, exposing his coffee and tobacco-stained teeth. "But let me tell you, she was a beauty—still is, I guess. Did you know she and Mindy coulda passed for sisters? Or twins, even? Some of the older guys called the two of them 'The Bobbsey Twins.' Not sure who that was, maybe a cartoon or video game or something. The problem was, though, I never could...."

"Okay," I said, cutting him off. I had heard enough, painfully recalling that sometimes it's best not to ask questions if you are not sure you really want to hear the answer.

CHAPTER 23

Between the professor, George Martin, and the construction worker, Carlton Lee, I had learned a lot. They were at different ends of the social, educational and economic spectrum, yet both seemed attracted to Mindy. The common thread from her end appeared to be money. Both could, and did, offer her that. She, in turn, appeared to have sent much of it to help support her mother. It was a strange and puzzling series of connections.

And Jenna, the woman I loved, the person I thought I wanted to spend the rest of my life with…. The more I heard, the less certain I was that I really knew her. She appeared to have been honest about her past, to a certain degree anyway. She didn't volunteer information, or describe past situations, but didn't try to deny them if asked. If she knew about it, and what went on there, why had she not mentioned Mindy's "farm"? Many years ago, when I was younger, I once heard my grandfather describe someone as an "onion": "Just when you think you've got to know them, another layer peels off." I was beginning to think the description fit Jenna. The time would come to face this with her, to have an open and honest discussion, but that was in the future. For the time being, I would continue to work on Mindy's case.

The fourth person on my abbreviated interview list was Mindy's brother, Daniel Peter Davis, Jr., MD, FACC. I did my due diligence before trying to contact him, a Google search, a review of any malpractice cases or criminal offenses listed on the Georgia Composite Medical Board website, or anything else of an untoward nature. He came up clean. His LinkedIn profile detailed his academic background and medical training. He appeared to be at or near the top in everything he did: Phi Beta Kappa at the University of Georgia; a third-year Alpha Omega Alpha inductee in medical school; a coveted fellowship in Internal Medicine and Interventional Cardiology at the Cleveland Clinic. His Facebook page suggested that in addition to all this, he was a family man with a lovely wife and two cute kids. After completion of his medical training, he'd been recruited by the premier cardiology group in Savannah, rapidly becoming known for his skill and expertise. Peter Davis, Jr. had done everything right. There was no doubt that he had made his mother proud, seeming to have washed away the stain of his parents' modest upbringings. Other than a few brief words exchanged at Mindy's memorial service, Peter and I had never met. I doubted he would remember me other than in the context of the guy that accompanied Jenna to the event.

Not knowing where to start, I called Dr. Davis's office and asked the receptionist to please deliver a message to the doctor, giving him my name, cell phone number, and the message that I was working with the Savannah police in regard to his sister's death. If I had not heard back from him in a day or two, I'd try another way of getting in touch. To my surprise, he called me back within fifteen minutes.

Dr. Davis was cordial, said that he remembered meeting me with Jenna, and had been told by his mother that I'd probably be calling to speak with him. He sounded grateful, saying he "wasn't sure how I can be of help, but I'll do just about anything necessary to find Mindy's killer. I want to apologize if my mother was a bit negative or in any way uncooperative. She's quite bitter about a lot of things, with my father's early death and then the loss of my sister."

"I understand completely," I said. "And I want to be clear that I can't make you any promises, other than I will do my best. My involvement was Jenna's idea originally, and the Savannah police welcomed a fresh set of eyes."

"I know, and I appreciate—we all appreciate—your efforts," the doctor said, sounding genuinely grateful. "I have some time this coming weekend if you're free to talk then. We can meet at my house, or anywhere in town here that's convenient. I'm on second back-up call, which means I have to stay in the area, but the likelihood of my having to go in for an emergency is small." I told him the weekend would be fine. We decided to meet Saturday afternoon at his house on Skidaway Island. He gave me the address and his private cell number if anything came up. Dr. Davis seemed eager to cooperate.

At 2:45 on Saturday afternoon I gave my name and the purpose of my visit to the attendant at the gatehouse guarding the entrance to Dr. Davis's subdivision. He had left my name and the approximate time of my arrival; I was given directions and ushered right through. The neighborhood was filled with million-dollar homes set in a forest of live oak, visual statements of wealth and success at whatever endeavor the owners had undertaken. The Davis house, a two-story brick Georgian design with a circular driveway in front, vaguely resembled the home of the elder Mrs. Davis in Vidalia. Dr. Davis answered the door, informally dressed in a loose-fitting Hawaiian-patterned shirt, Bermuda shorts and sandals. He shook my hand, smiled and apologized for his informal garb, explaining he was "just taking it easy on the weekend."

"It's a nice day; let's sit out back," he suggested, leading me to a comfortably furnished lanai next to a large swimming pool in the back yard. He motioned me to a chair and sat down opposite, saying, "Tell me how I can be of help to you."

"I wish I knew," I said, "but this is an unusual situation. The investigation into your sister's death has stalled, despite the earnest efforts of multiple law enforcement agencies and dozens of investigators over a period of years. I was asked to take a fresh look at things, not because I have some special expertise, but in part because I do not. I practiced law at one time, and now I am primarily an art dealer. I'm working on Mindy's case as a special investigator for the Savannah/Chatham County police. And Mindy's friend, Jenna, is a close friend of mine. I'm doing this in part because of her."

Davis watched me intently as I spoke, then said, "I know all that. I checked on your credentials when you interviewed my mother. I know you're legit." He appeared confident and in charge.

Sensing the situation, I thought I would let him take the lead. "So, where would you like to start? I know this has been with you for years; are there things or areas of investigation that you believe deserve a closer look, or have not been properly investigated?"

"Possibly. I wish I could be more specific, but one thing that has been on my mind since they found Mindy's remains is the apparent viciousness of her death. The autopsy report—as limited as it was—suggested she was beaten and strangled. I am not totally sure there has been a focus on those who were angry with her, or jealous of her, or had other emotions that would lead to such a violent event. I believe it's pretty obvious that she was not killed where she was buried, so there's no crime scene that might yield clues to help point in one direction or another. Have you thought about that aspect?"

"It would appear to be a good path to investigate," I said, neutrally. "Tell me more."

In truth, the idea had been mentioned, but in reviewing the files, no one seemed to have suggested that specific approach. Davis was saying, in essence, that the violent nature of her death suggested there had to be a preexisting connection of some sort between Mindy and her killer. Look at those with a connection and think about where they both might have been. It was a great idea to be sure, but her murder had taken place years before. Even if one knew that location, the passage of time would likely have erased the evidence.

"I wish I could be more specific, but I can't," Davis continued. "Mindy didn't live in a bubble. She was gregarious, had lots of friends, both male and female, and unfortunately had gotten into drugs…," he stopped mid-sentence, then continued, "…and was probably taking money from men for—how do I say this politely?—'other things' as well. She was one of the main attractions in that so-called 'club' where she worked, and she could have made enemies there—some of the other girls, for example. Or maybe one of the patrons she clashed with? I don't know."

"Your mother seemed quite upset about Mindy's lifestyle."

"She was, and still is, even though Mindy was doing her best to help after our dad died. I was off doing my training at the time and could barely make ends meet. She honestly saved our mother from bankruptcy. Our mom should be grateful, but…." Davis didn't finish his sentence.

"Your mother mentioned that you two inherited a piece of land from your father, an old farm I think she said. Was that ever an issue?" I asked.

I saw a dark look flash across Davis's face before he answered. "Not really. To be exact, it was eighty-three acres and was my father's family's farm. When he died, his will left it to both Mindy and me, but with the proviso that if there was any income from the property or if it was sold during my mother's lifetime, the proceeds would go to her. We paid for the upkeep and taxes, and she got a little money occasionally from hunting leases. I wanted to sell it, but Mindy was insistent that we not. I didn't have much use for the property, my mother didn't want to sell it because it had been my dad's, and Mindy would occasionally spend some time there. It's mine now after her death, but I don't have time to go there much at all. A guy who lives down the road looks in on it for me."

Davis's answer did not exactly fit with what Carlton Lee had said. Maybe he didn't know about the "parties." Maybe he was downplaying it like his mother, embarrassed by his sister's iniquities.

CHAPTER 24

We spoke for the better part of an hour or more. Davis was friendly, informal and, as closely as I could approximate, trying to be helpful with the investigation. He invited me to stay for dinner and meet his wife and kids. I thanked him but politely declined, making an excuse about transcribing my notes while they were still fresh in my mind. On thinking about my visit, the only small thing that seemed out of place was Davis's reaction when I'd asked about the farm, but even then I wasn't totally certain that he was responding negatively to my question. Something that he brought up, and one thing I thought I needed to follow up next, was his take on some sort of a negative relationship between Mindy and her killer. I didn't have access to the files at police headquarters over the weekend, so I put off working on that till Monday. In the meantime, I needed to see Jenna, both to refresh my soul with her company, and to ask her what she knew about the Davis farm.

It was late in the day when I called, but Jenna was home and sounded eager to see me. "You've been so busy lately. I thought you'd forgotten me," she said, slightly giggly.

"How could I?" I asked, playfully.

"When are you free? It's Saturday, Robert is spending the night at a friend's house, and I'm home all by myself watching reruns on Netflix."

"How about I take you out to dinner?" I asked.

"I'll be ready when you show up," she said and hung up. I picked her up an hour later. We ate at a Mexican restaurant in Pembroke, and were back at her place before nine. As we settled in on the couch she said, "We've gone all evening without mentioning the investigation. How's that going?"

"Good, I guess. No great discoveries. But that reminds me, I was interviewing one of the guys that hung out at the club and knew Mindy, and he said something about Mindy's farm up near the church where the memorial service was held. Do you know anything about that?" Quite deliberately, I didn't say the "guy" was Carl, the same one she had slapped, or that I'd asked Mindy's brother more or less the same question.

Like Peter Davis, a brief scowl passed across Jenna's face before she answered. "Yeah, I thought we talked about that. When their father died, Mindy and her brother inherited a small farm in the country up near I-16. She took me there several times. It wasn't very big, an old farmhouse, a barn or two, that sort of thing. She kinda used it as a getaway place. I don't think her brother was there much at all, but then he was off getting his medical training around that time."

"He said something about Mindy having 'parties' there, about...."

"Yeah," Jenna said, stopping me mid-sentence. "That went on." She looked down. I did not have to ask more to understand what her reaction meant.

"Do you think that, or anything connected to what went on there, might have had any relation to her murder?"

Jenna was still staring at her hands. She responded with a weak, "No, probably not." She then looked up and said, "About the only really strange thing happened one Sunday morning. There had been a crowd there the night before and two or three guys stayed over—I think they got too drunk to drive home. I remember one of them slept in the barn. Anyway, about ten o'clock Peter Davis drove in the yard. No one, especially

Mindy, knew he was coming. He saw the cars parked out front and he and Mindy got in a huge fight shouting at one another. I was inside and watching through the window. He never saw me. Peter started to come in the house, but Mindy stopped him, yelling and saying she was entertaining some friends, and she owned as much of the place as he did, and he couldn't just barge in like that and so on. She shoved him and he shoved her back and then turned around got in his car and left." Peter's mother had not spoken of any discord over the farm property. The episode appeared to be a relatively minor spat between siblings, the sort of thing that happens in many families. Their mother was the only one who still seemed to harbor ill feelings.

I started to ask Jenna more about the "parties," about what went on, but thought better of it. On one hand I thought I knew enough, and on the other I realized I probably did not want to learn more, at least from Jenna's perspective. Between us, the past was the past and had to remain so. But I was still curious. I didn't think speaking with Peter Davis in more detail would be helpful. I decided to get back in touch with Carl Lee, or perhaps one of the other men who had appeared on the list as club patrons.

On Monday morning at nine o'clock I was once more back in the small room at police headquarters, digging through the files in search of a new candidate to interview. Carl Lee was one of four "club patrons" who had been interviewed twice. I had a good idea that he was likely to know the three others, and I wanted his advice as to who might give me more insight to the farm and Mindy's parties. I called his cell and got his voicemail. He returned my call about an hour and a half later. "Mr. O'Toole," he said with a friendly voice. "What can I do for you?"

"I want to follow up on what went on at Mindy's farm. I appreciate what you told me, but I was wondering if anyone else might be willing to talk with me. There were three people besides you who attended the memorial service and were later interviewed. Do you know any of them that also went to one of the parties at the farm?"

"For sure," Lee said. "There were Jim Tyson, Sonny Gibson, and a third guy, goes by Larry, but I'm not sure I remember his last name."

I looked at the interview list. "Maybe Lawrence Wright? Larry's a common nickname for that."

"Yeah, that's it, Larry Wright."

"So, of the three, which do you recommend I talk with?"

"Well, not Sonny, because he just got remarried and if you start bringing up things from the past, there's gonna be trouble. I didn't know Larry that well, but Jim Tyson's been a good friend for years, and he was at Mindy's parties more than me. And he's a straight-shooting guy. You want me to feel him out, see if he'll be willing to talk with you?"

"That would be good. I have his contact numbers…."

"I do, too. I'll get back to you." Lee hung up. Forty-five minutes later he called back. "Sure, Jim's willing to talk, but you gotta kinda keep it private. He's married, too, and don't want his wife to find out about what he sometimes does in his spare time."

"I understand." Lee gave me Tyson's cell number and told me to call now if I wanted to. Tyson answered on the second ring. I introduced myself and told him briefly why I wanted to talk with him.

"No problem," Tyson said, "You just gotta keep this on the q.t. Don't want what I do in private to become public."

"I can promise you that. I'll only need about half an hour of your time."

"Okay, I can meet you after work today if you want. You can come by the business and we'll talk after everyone's gone home." He said he worked as the manager at a building supply store. He gave me the address and told me to wait until about five minutes before the six o'clock closing time to walk in. By six-fifteen we were sitting in Tyson's small office wedged between a rack of pre-hung doors and stacks of laminate flooring. He appeared to be in his late forties, a man used to being in charge. "Let's get one thing straight before we start. I wouldn't be talking with you at all if Carl Lee hadn't vouched for you. I've got a lot to lose if my wife finds out some things, or if my name crops up where it shouldn't be. I understand this is off the record and just to help you out maybe in figuring out who killed Mindy." He paused, waiting for my response. I told him I understood completely and agreed to his conditions. "So, what can I help you with…?" he said.

"Carl said you went to one or more of Mindy's 'parties' over in Toombs County north of Vidalia. I don't know if you are aware that the examination of her remains showed that she likely had been pretty severely beaten and strangled. The investigators think that suggests that whoever killed her had some kind of relationship with her that had gone bad. For example, a boyfriend who found her cheating, or something like that. I'm trying to understand if there was anyone or anything that might point to one or more persons who could have done something like that and then hid her body, hoping to avoid being caught."

Tyson chuckled, "Well, you can rule out the boyfriend part right away. Mindy was a beautiful, intelligent, and well-educated person, but for a handful of cash, she could be—and was—anybody's girlfriend. I never quite figured that out.... Such a waste. I really liked her—cared for her even. It was more than just sex."

"I think the investigators believe she was on drugs. Do you think that had anything to do with it. Maybe something with her dealer, or the like?"

"Again, not likely. There was a little marijuana smoking around, but she catered to an older crowd. It's the kids that are more into weed. Now, I think she was into meth, but I'm not completely certain. You can tell how people act when they're high on meth. I'm pretty sure she wasn't shooting up or smoking it, but I'd suspect she was swallowing the crap. Folks get kinda euphoric, jumpy, agitated." He paused. "That was her. But not all the time."

"You never saw her get in an argument with anyone?"

"Just one time. Mostly I saw Mindy at the club, or someplace we'd go to be alone. I went to one of her parties at the farm, had a bit too much to drink and ended up sleeping there. The next morning I woke up with a hell of a hangover and heard this yelling going on out in front of the house. She and some guy were having at it, accusing each other of this and that—I really couldn't hear all they were saying, but they were upset. And he said something to the effect he was gonna come inside and see who's there, and she pushes him back to stop him. So then he pushes her—knocks her down, really, and gets in his car and leaves. I didn't ask any questions and don't know who the guy was. That's about all I know about that."

CHAPTER 25

I drove back to the gallery and my apartment, a stream of possible scenarios playing out in my head. Both Jenna and Jim Tyson had observed Mindy get into what sounded like a minor physical spat with someone. Jenna identified the person as her brother, Peter. While perhaps disturbing, what family hasn't seen occasional disputes between siblings? That certainly did not make him a suspect, but it was just another confusing fact in a complicated story. I realized I needed help, some objective perspective on what I'd found so far. I resolved to get in touch with Jack Garrett the next morning to see if he could help me get my thoughts in order.

Promptly at 8:00 a.m. I called Jack's cell. He seemed pleased to hear from me, and said he could meet me at police headquarters at ten that morning. "Retirement can get kinda boring," he observed. We sat in the small conference room while I went over what I'd done since we last talked. "Sounds like you've been busy," Garrett commented. "In a way, you've confirmed what was already known, and dug up a couple of new things that may or may not be important. Personally, I'm not really surprised at what either Mindy's mother or brother had to say. They were the two people closest to her, and the ones who'd want the most to know what really happened. In these situations, many times family members will show signs of bitterness—of anger even—and sometimes it's directed at the victim. Why did she get herself killed? It must have been something she did to cause this great sadness—that sort of thing. But the brother, the doctor, seemed to be a bit more level-headed, I take it?" I said it seemed that way.

"The episode of Mindy and Peter getting into it when he found she was having 'parties'—I believe that's what you called them—at their jointly owned property is not that surprising. I wouldn't make much of it, but I wouldn't forget it either. The professor, Martin, is clearly a nut. You can't rule him out, but I just can't see him as the killer, even if he is left-handed. Let's back off a minute and think about the basics here again.

"First, we talked about motive, means and opportunity, and again, since we know how Mindy died, we're looking for motive and opportunity. The second of those two, opportunity, translates to where the murder occurred, in other words, the crime scene. Those two things, the why and the where, have totally eluded the cops that have worked this case for years now. I'd say at this point, you need to focus everything on one or both of them, as they are often connected.

"The second thing is to do some thinking outside the box. We've been assuming that Mindy was killed by someone she knew or had some contact with, given the violent nature of her death. But there are the outliers, the random murders of serial killers, for example. I'm sure it's been a while since the investigators ran an NCIC search. Have you looked into doing that again?"

"No…, I hate to admit it, but I'm not really sure what that is…."

"Okay, a brief history. The National Crime Information Center—NCIC—is the name for a series of digital databases maintained by the FBI. The original setup dates back to J. Edgar Hoover in the late 1960s, and of course there have been numerous expansions and upgrades. What you'd be looking for are crimes with similar characteristics, and probably ones limited to this region, say Georgia or the Southeast. Every police department of any size usually has an NCIC-trained person. You can search by the nature of the crime, the MO, the type of victim, and so on. And there are tie-ins to a number of similar state databases. So, for example, if you came up with several situations where a young woman had been beaten and strangled, and her body buried in a shallow grave, all in a two-year period, you might be looking for a serial killer. A lot of times a search is not helpful, but it's worth a look."

"Let's do it then," I said. Garrett volunteered to find out the name of the current NCIC person and have him or her contact me. We continued talking for nearly another hour, speculating, discussing possible situations that might have surrounded Mindy's death, but in the end came up with nothing new.

Garrett left, and I was considering finding lunch when I heard a knock at the conference room door. I opened it to see a young woman in a police uniform. She smiled, stuck out her hand and said, "I'm Corporal Yates, the NCIC officer. Detective Garrett said you might want me to run a NCIC search." It took me a moment to react. Corporal Yates appeared barely out of her teens.

"Uh…, yeah. I wasn't expecting someone so quickly."

"He said it was important, and whatever Detective Garrett says usually gets done quickly. He's retired, but still a legend around here." Yates looked around the room, focusing on the stack of eight boxes. "What can I help you with?"

"I'm working on a cold case, the Mindy Davis murder. Jack—Detective Garrett—said an NCIC search might prove helpful."

"Sure," she said. "I guess you've already searched the files in these boxes?"

"Yes, I've spent many, many hours poring over them. Making notes, that kind of...."

"No, I mean digitally. We scan in almost everything now. Makes reviewing old cases *so* much easier." She stressed the "so."

"I'll have to get you to help me do that," I said, "but first, I want to follow up on Detective Garrett's suggestion about an NCIC search."

Perhaps thinking she was dealing with a digital Luddite, Corporal Yates, who insisted that I address her by her given name, Lauren, gave me a brief overview of the system and how it works. "To be honest, it's kind of nebulous, not the clean, crisp sort of thing that you'd expect from a well-organized relational database. That's probably because it was originally conceived and set up in the dark ages, like before my parents were born, back when my granddaddy was a cop here in Savannah. But it helps, sometimes." She said she had a master's degree in information technology. For a moment, I felt very old. Going back and forth, we came up with a series of key words defining what we were searching for. Lauren said she'd start by limiting the search to Georgia and the adjacent states, Florida, the Carolinas, Tennessee and Alabama, looking for crimes that occurred in the last decade. "That should give us an idea of the kind of info we'll find." It would probably be the next day before she had any results.

At ten the next morning I was back in the conference room, going through the material generated after the discovery of Mindy's remains, when I heard a knock at the door. It was Lauren, clutching a sheaf of papers. "Got some hits, but I'm not sure how helpful they'll be." I cleared off a spot and she laid them on the table. "There are a number of vaguely similar crimes that have occurred over the last ten years. Young women get murdered for all sorts of reasons, but most are done by boyfriends and other close associates. And most of these get solved quickly. One set of variants I searched for was unsolved killings of females in the eighteen to twenty-eight age range, in which an effort had been made to hide the body, and that occurred within fifty miles of a city with a larger college or university. Yesterday, we talked about Martin, the weird professor guy. You said he taught at Georgia Southern in Statesboro for a while, and Mindy's body was found in Bulloch County, the same place. I found two other unsolved killings that happened to undergraduate students at the University of Georgia in Athens, and at Georgia College in Milledgeville. In both situations, there were suspects, but insufficient evidence to make an arrest. But…" she paused, "…Dr. Martin or Martinez had lectured or taught a course in each school around the time of the murders. And I want you to know it took a lot of digging to find that out that last bit of information." Lauren sounded proud of herself.

"Gosh! That sounds interesting."

"I have to tell you these are just preliminary hits. Many times—a lot of times, in fact—these fall apart when investigators take a closer look at the facts. I'm excited and glad to work with you on this case, but please don't lose focus. In the year or so I've been doing this, I've discovered that sometimes we put too much faith in digital things. All of the results are not in yet, but I couldn't wait to tell you that bit of news. I'll let you know when I have more."

CHAPTER 26

I had no idea how to interpret Lauren's findings. Professors teach at universities and, sadly, murders occur. From somewhere in the past I recalled an instructor I'd had in college warn the class about the difference between association and causation. Just because two things are found to occur together, it doesn't necessarily mean that one caused the other. Lauren seemed to know her field though, and I needed to pay attention to anything she found of interest. At this point, it appeared the single new revelation that had come out of my interviews and review of the case was the fact that Mindy had used the farm she and her brother inherited to entertain men from the club, apparently for the purpose of making money. I wanted to have a look at the place, even if the only clear reason I could find to justify it was simple curiosity. Jenna admitted she'd been there. She would know how to find it. I called her at work.

"Are you sure you want to go way over there? It's at least a forty-five-minute drive from Claxton and probably twice that from your place in Savannah." Jenna was not eager.

"I know, and yes, I do want to see the place. I'm trying to dig into this case, and the 'farm' or whatever it is keeps coming up."

"Okay," she said, sounding hesitant. "This Saturday will be the first time I can get away for several hours. Would you mind picking me up here at my apartment? I'll arrange a sitter for Robert." I said I'd be there at ten.

Jeanna was standing out front, waiting for me when I arrived. The first thing she said after getting in my car was, "You realize I'm not excited about this."

"I know. I was picking up on that yesterday when I called. But it's something new that apparently hadn't come up in the investigation before and at the least, it deserves a look."

"Okay," she said and remained silent as we got on the road. Turning north in Vidalia, we followed a two-lane paved highway for ten minutes or so, passing through vast tracts of planted pines interspersed with the occasional singlewide or modest home set on roadside lots. Jenna pointed to a well-maintained dirt road that turned off into the forest to the east. After about two miles we came to what appeared to be a large hayfield, in the middle of which on a slight rise sat a wood-framed farmhouse with a series of barns and outbuildings. "Here we are," Jenna said. "You can just drive on up and park in front of the house."

"Kind of in the middle of nowhere," I observed.

"Like, yeah," she responded, then folded her arms over her chest and continued, "I'm really uncomfortable being here. Too many bad memories…." She didn't finish her sentence. "I think I'll just stay in the car. You can walk around and check things out, and then we'll go. Okay?"

"Okay," I said, feeling bad about putting her in this situation. I got out of the car and surveyed the house. It was old, dating from the sharecropping days and the Great Depression of the early twentieth century. The gabled roof was covered with galvanized tin, faded to a neutral shade of gray that matched a peeling paint job of approximately the same color. Built on a slope and facing downhill, the front porch was accessed by a worn-looking set of wooden stairs with a handrail on each side. Two brick chimneys must have been the primary source of heat at one time, but I noted a relatively new HVAC compressor suggesting modern air conditioning. A moderate-sized barn with interior animal stalls loomed in the back yard, next to a small fenced enclosure—for hogs? A gate in a barbed wire fence led to a several-acre pasture in the rear. What appeared to be an abandoned outhouse stood forlornly next to the hog pen. I half expected a character from a Walker Evans photo to pull back a curtain and peer at me through the window.

I was just headed back to the front of the house when I saw a run-down looking pickup turn into the drive leading to the house, flying up to a sudden stop in a cloud of dust. An older man, perhaps in his late sixties or seventies, hopped out, eyeing me with suspicion. He was dressed in faded khaki and boots and wore a black leather belt with a large caliber revolver protruding from a holster on his right hip. "Howya doin'?" he said in a not unfriendly voice.

"Fine, thank you, and you?" I replied, returning the courtesy.

"You know this is private property? Ain't nobody supposed to be up here around the house." His hand hovered within easy reach of his gun.

"Yes, I know," I said while trying to appear friendly. "I understand it belongs to Dr. Davis."

"You know him?" The hovering hand seemed to relax.

"Yes, we've met."

"He send you here?"

"Not directly, but I'm investigating his sister's murder."

"You a cop?"

"I'm working as an investigator with the Savannah police," I replied, not directly answering the question. "I'm John O'Toole." The reply seemed to satisfy him.

The man stepped forward and extended his hand. "I'm Billy Barlow, retired from the Toombs County Sheriff's Department. I live just down the road there and keep an eye on this place for Dr. Davis. Maybe you didn't notice, but there's a bunch of cameras around." He pointed at two nearby camouflaged game cameras mounted in trees above eye level. "They send me a photo if something triggers a motion alarm." He pushed his pistol back firmly in the holster. "So what are you doing way up here? Poor Mindy went missing years ago, but I heard they recently found where her body had been buried over in Bulloch County."

"We're taking a fresh look at the investigation, trying to see if anything was missed. I understand Mindy used to entertain up here sometimes."

"Yeah, drinking parties they were. I was patrolling back then. We arrested several guys for DUI. And I remember having a talk with the girl about not creating a public nuisance. Nobody really cares way out here in the country, but still, some of those guys would try to drive home when they shouldn't be."

"Do you have any thoughts about what might have happened to Mindy?" I asked. "She just didn't show up for work one day, and no one seems to know where she was or what she was doing for several days before that."

"Well, I know she was up here not too long before she went missing. I don't remember the exact dates and all that, but I told somebody about it back then—it's been several years and I done forgot the details." Barlow scratched his head. "It seems like it took several weeks to figure out something bad might have happened to her. And 'course, nobody really knew for sure she was dead till they found her bones."

"That's interesting. I hadn't heard that."

"As I recall, she and Dr. Davis owned the place together. He was off in school or something for the longest, and Mindy pretty much had run of the place. That's about all I know."

I thanked him, and said we would be on our way. Barlow said, "I guess I need to tell Dr. Davis I saw you here. You seem like a good fella and I hate to ask, but would you mind showing me some ID?"

"Not at all." I pulled out the Savannah/Chatham police "Investigator" card bearing my photo and gave it to him.

Barlow studied it briefly and handed it back. "And who's your lady friend over there in the car? She looks kinda familiar, sort of reminds me a bit of Mindy." He walked over toward my vehicle, stopped, and squinted in the window. Looking back at me, he said with a note of surprise, "Is that Candi? Haven't seen her in years and years."

Jenna, who'd heard the exchange, buried her face in her hands and began sobbing.

CHAPTER 27

I could not find the words to apologize to Jenna. She had done so very much for me, standing by me with her love and support in my darkest hours and here I was, dragging her on an expedition prompted by my own selfish curiosity. All I could do was say, "I'm sorry."

"It's not you, John," she replied, looking at me through tear-stained eyes. "It's me—or who I was, my past really—I can't escape it. I was the one who pushed you to look into what happened to Mindy. I'll be all right. Time will heal me, but in the meantime, please don't feel like you should share the shame for my mistakes." It was an elegant statement, one of acknowledgment and acceptance, but it did not lessen Jenna's pain. I reached out to hold her hand, keeping it covered with mine until we reached her home.

Back at the solitude of my apartment, I sifted through the memories of the day. The visit seemed to produce no obvious surprises or unanswered questions, at least as far as I could tell without looking inside the farmhouse. But, remembering Jack Garrett's warnings about violations of the Fourth and Fourteenth Amendments, that could not even be considered without a search warrant approved by a judge. I wanted to keep that option open in case things changed.

The following day, a Sunday, passed quietly. I called Jenna to check on her. She said she was doing "fine," thanked me for my offer to come spend time with her, but said she'd rather see me later in the week when she felt better. On Monday morning, I was back in the conference room, determined this time to take another look at the interviews done in the weeks that followed Mindy's disappearance. As it would turn out, an interview that was *not* done would prove to be of importance.

Reviewing the investigators' notes, it seemed clear that it was a full two weeks after Mindy's contact with the world ceased before it was fully realized that she might be, or more likely was, a victim of foul play. She was an intelligent independent young woman, well-educated, self-supporting, and probably not too close to her mother who disapproved of her lifestyle, or her brother who at the time was living in Ohio doing a cardiology fellowship. So, the initial interviews and fact-seeking inquiries were directed at her friends and associates, people she hung out with, worked with, or knew in various other capacities. The investigators, most of whom were officers of the Savannah/Chatham police force, kept excellent notes, recording not only factual items, but also speculation, gossip, accusations, innuendo and pretty much anything else pertinent to Mindy's life, work, interest, friends and so on. The interviews included Jenna's, but hers was not among the first as she was in rehab at the time.

One document, which I'd reviewed before, became all the more interesting to me now that I had gained a better understanding of the process. It was a master list of persons that the detectives and other investigators thought should be interviewed in the case. Several pages long, the names were listed in a column on the left, followed by their relationship to Mindy—such as "Friend," "Club Employee," or the like—and the date of the interview once completed. I had not paid much attention to it before, preferring to read the individual interview reports themselves. Now looking again at the master list, I ran my finger down the left-hand column, stopping suddenly at the name of Brandon Wiggins. His relationship was listed in the next column as "Boyfriend?" but in the usual box listing the date of his interview the word "Deceased" was written. Obviously, there were no records of an interview that did not take place. This was something I had missed earlier. Who was Brandon Wiggins and what was his actual relationship to Mindy? If he were in fact her "boyfriend," why had I not seen it mentioned elsewhere?

At just that moment, Lauren knocked on the door, entered and sat down, looking somewhat disappointed. "What's up?" I asked.

"Aw, bummer," she said. "Remember what I said about the murders and the art professor last week? I was really stoked about that, and over the weekend spent a lot of hours running some simulations, looking at the data in different ways. Well, I don't think there is any connection at all between the two events. In fact the probability of finding that association came up with p-values ranging from a high of 0.42 to a low of 0.23, so...."

"Whoa! You lost me there at 'p-value.' Would you mind putting it in terms an art dealer or attorney can understand," I said.

"Just this: Ignore what I said last week. Let's look elsewhere."

I held up the master list of potential interviewees. "I just found something strange here. It's a list of persons to be interviewed that was compiled not long after Mindy went missing. The investigators appear to have spoken with essentially everyone on the list, but with one prominent exception. Just here," I pointed to Brandon Wiggins's name, "is someone who is listed as Mindy's 'boyfriend'—with a question mark—but was not interviewed because he was said to be dead. It doesn't make sense. Can you track that down and maybe figure out what's going on here?"

Lauren sat up, her expression eager. "Absolutely! I'll try to have you something by tomorrow morning." She rose as if to leave.

"I think you'll need to do some digging in these boxes if...." I started.

"Why in the world would I want to do that? All of that stuff has been scanned. I'll start with a keyword search and go from there. Turn hours into minutes." She grinned, saying over her shoulder as she left, "See you tomorrow, if not before."

That left me hanging. Who was this guy, Brandon, and why had his name not come up before in the investigation? I knew Lauren would track it down, but again curiosity got the best of me. I pushed the stack of papers aside and took my iPad out of my briefcase. Brandon was said to be deceased, so I began by searching for "Brandon Wiggins" and "obituary." The first hit was from the *Advance*, the local weekly newspaper covering Toombs, Montgomery and Wheeler Counties. It answered a few questions but raised even more. Wiggins was born, raised and had still been living near Vidalia. He was a graduate of Vidalia High School, had earned a degree in Forest Management from the University of Georgia, and was married to the former Anna Everett. His parents and several siblings were listed, but there was no mention of any children. Based on his stated age, he appeared to be four or five years older than Mindy, which would have made him a contemporary of Peter Davis, also a graduate of Vidalia High. The write-up referred to Wiggins's "tragic death," the details of which were not given. It appeared that there was no funeral per se, but rather a memorial service held at the First United Methodist Church in Vidalia.

Searching further I came across digital versions of several news accounts, all with the basic headline of "Local Man Missing—Feared Dead," or something similar. Although the writeups varied, the core facts remained the same. It appeared that Wiggins was an avid fisherman, especially in the Altamaha River, which forms the southern border of Toombs County. He often went camping overnight near the river, rising early the next morning to be on the water near sunrise when the fish were more likely to bite. His pickup truck was found near the river at a public boat ramp but his boat, which he usually hauled in the bed of his truck, was missing. When his wife could not reach him on his cell phone and he did not return home near the end of the day, a search was begun by the local emergency responders. His boat, with his fishing gear in it, was discovered approximately three miles downriver from his truck. There was no sign of Wiggins. The search was continued for a number of following days, but it was assumed by authorities that he had fallen out of the boat and drowned. The possibility that he could have been attacked and consumed by an alligator was not mentioned. The memorial service had taken place four weeks later.

Wiggins's presumed fate was tragic, but the most intriguing thing from my perspective was the timing of his disappearance. Combining the details from the several online accounts, his wife, Anna, stated that Wiggins worked as a forester and loved to be outdoors. "Relaxing for him was being in the woods," she said, and added that he would often spend the night at the river, sleeping in the back of his truck and getting up early the next morning to fish. She had last spoken with him around midday on a Saturday, and called the local sheriff worried about his whereabouts when she had not heard from him by late Sunday afternoon. All of this occurred on the same weekend that Mindy went missing.

CHAPTER 28

I was back in the conference room at police headquarters early the next morning, eager to chase down what appeared to be a new lead. The evening before, I had called Jenna, hoping that she might shed some light on the relationship between Mindy and Brandon Wiggins. The reference to him as her "boyfriend" appeared to be unique in the case files, occurring only once on the interview sheet where I found it. "Brandon?" Jenna said, sounding puzzled. "I don't remember anyone by that name at the club, but then it's been a good while. Lots of guys came and went, and unless they stood out or did something special—or stupid—most were easy to forget. And, too, remember that I wasn't there in the weeks before Mindy disappeared." I was hoping Jenna would know more.

Lauren dropped by just after 9:00 a.m. "I'm making progress," she said, "but I need to get my hands on some things before I'm ready to talk about it. I hope to have something this afternoon."

"What are you looking for?" I asked.

"A high school yearbook. Several of them, in fact." She left without saying more.

The problem, it seemed to me, was drawing connections. In reality, Mindy seemed to have few close relationships. She had friends, of course, including Jenna, and was a very public figure at the club. But I suspected most knew little or nothing about her private life, her needs, her wants and her desires. She was of the age when many people, both men and women, thought of marriage and a family, something that had been on *my* mind for months. And how did Brandon fit into this picture? Was he truly her "boyfriend," or was this a speculative assumption used to fill a box on the interview form? He was married, of course. Were they simply having an affair, or was there more? Clearly, he was not the only man in her life. Was he aware and tolerant of the others? Too many questions; not enough answers.

My thoughts were interrupted by the buzzing of my cell phone. I glanced at the screen. It was Peter Davis's private number. I answered with a friendly "hello," assuming the doctor was calling to ask how the investigation was going, or to offer his assistance if needed. Instead I was greeted with a harsh, "I heard from Billy Barlow. He said you and your female friend were poking around my house in Toombs County. Listen here, Mr. O'Toole, and listen well. That is private property. I am the sole owner and I guard my privacy. I know you call yourself investigating my sister's death, but that unfortunate event has nothing whatsoever to do with the place. So, if you don't mind, keep your nose where it belongs. And if you're foolish enough to ignore my warning, you will suffer the consequences." Having spewed his vitriol, Davis hung up without waiting for my reply.

Dr. Davis's call only served to add another layer of fog to the case. Why did he react so angrily? Yes, I probably should have told him in advance I wanted to see "the farm," and yes, I was technically trespassing, but he knew I was engaged in the investigation, and had been generous in offering his help when we first met. Perhaps he was like his mother, bitter and angry, but had carefully hidden it behind a façade of gentility and professionalism.

Just at that moment Lauren arrived back at the door, this time carrying four bulky books which she flopped on the table.

"Okay, I think maybe I've found something, but I don't know if it's going to be helpful to you." Pointing at the books, "These are yearbooks from Vidalia High School that cover the four years when Brandon Wiggins was in the ninth through twelfth grades. Looks like he was, I think they call it—a 'good ol' boy'—drove a pickup, loved hunting and fishing, that kind of thing. He was a member, and in fact the president during his senior year, of the FFA, the Future Farmers of America—you know—the guys that wore those navy blue jackets with the yellow patch on the front? And in his 'Senior Statement' he said he was going to UGA and become a forester. Here's a picture of him." She held up a page in the yearbook for me to see. A ruggedly handsome, dark-haired teenager stared back from the page. Though the image was in black and white, the logo of the FFA could clearly be seen on his jacket over his left breast.

"So that's Brandon?" I said.

"Yes, but there's more. Guess who he hung out with?"

"I have no idea."

Holding up a second page from the yearbook, I was surprised to see a younger image of none other than Peter Davis, Jr. Lauren pointed out several other group-shot photos of the Vidalia High senior class that showed the two of them in the same crowd. "They were classmates," Lauren said. "Graduated together. That's a connection."

"Yes, but…." I hesitated, wanting to get my thoughts together before I said more. "Vidalia is a small town. The two of them just happen to be the same age. It's not like they chose to enroll in the same school—they didn't have another choice. I wouldn't have expected to find anything different.

"I know, but from a data management perspective I'd say any possible connection needs to be explored," Lauren said.

"Think about it—someone's sister disappears one weekend and is discovered to be murdered. The same exact weekend, a high school classmate of the brother, who was alleged by someone to be her 'boyfriend' even though he was married to someone else, also disappears under what I'd call mysterious circumstances. They didn't ever find his body, did they?"

Lauren was right. I needed to adjust my thinking. "I tell you what let's do. I want to spend one more full day going through these files, seeing if there is something I've missed. You keep digging as well. And the day after tomorrow, I'll see if I can arrange to have both Jack Garrett and Pete Marsh meet us here to look at where we are, and make suggestions as to where we should go next. What do you think?"

"Sounds like a plan," Lauren said, smiling. "But," pointing at the eight boxes on the table, "you're going to try to dig through all this?"

"Not exactly, I've looked at everything at least once, but there are some things I want to focus on...."

"Do you have any idea how many pages of documents are in there?" she asked.

"I'm not really sure. I was guessing the first six boxes could have held maybe 30,000, but..."

"Okay, let's just take that number for a start. A lot of them—most of them maybe—are typed reports?"

"Yeah." I wasn't sure where she was going with this.

"Single- or double-spaced?"

"I don't know," I replied, beginning to get annoyed.

"We'll guess then with a lowball number, and say there are a total of 20,000 pages. A typed, single-spaced page holds about 500 words on average, so—if I'm figuring that correctly in my head —that's about ten million words you hope to review." She stopped and waited for my reply. The implication was obvious, so I said nothing. "All of this has been scanned and digitized," she continued. "I'll get to work on it and report back to you late tomorrow afternoon so we can plan what to say to the detectives."

For lack of a better response, I said, "Sounds good to me."

"Four o'clock tomorrow then, meet here?" I nodded. Lauren had taken charge.

I was beginning to feel a bit foolish, a rank amateur in a world of professionals, at least when it came to cold case investigation. And to be truthful, I was. I honestly had no idea where the search would lead, if anywhere. I was hoping to find some missing clue, some hidden and overlooked key that would unlock the truth. In a way, Lauren was being cruel, but she was right. My attempting to sift through thousands of pages of documents inscribed with millions of words—assuming her math was correct—almost rose to the level of silliness, a search for the proverbial needle in the haystack. But she was the expert in "information technology," affirmed by her graduate degree in the field. I was glad to have her assistance, even if it did mean swallowing my ego.

CHAPTER 29

I called both Pete Marsh and Jack Garrett, asking if they could meet with Lauren and me at 10:00 a.m. the day after next. Pete said he would need to rearrange his schedule, but promised to be there. Jack sounded eager to get a break from his greenhouses and flowers. I spent the remainder of the day sifting through the folders of the eight boxes, more determined than ever to find anything to say my hours spent cloistered in the sterility of the conference room had not been wasted. By five o'clock my eyes were beginning to glaze over and I was developing a slight headache. I had found nothing new. I decided to call it a day and head back to my apartment. The following day was the same. I read and reread reports, assessments, summaries, and suggestions for further investigation. I took another close look at the autopsy report on the examination of Mindy's remains and the crime scene investigation assessment of the site where they were discovered. I studied the photographs taken in her apartment by investigators after she was formally declared a missing person. All came to naught.

Shortly before our scheduled meeting time of 4:00 p.m., Lauren knocked and entered, a smile on her face and carrying several larger books. "Any progress?" she asked.

"I hate to admit it, but no. Nothing new. And you?"

"I think we're on to something," Lauren said, generously using the plural pronoun. "I've got a lead on this Brandon fellow, and just maybe some thoughts on where we might want to go from here."

"You're serious?" I asked, wondering what she had found or if this was the intro to a cruel joke.

"Very much so. First, let me apologize for yesterday. I know you've really put a lot into this case. My comments were stupid and inappropriate. You've spent hours and hours familiarizing yourself with the reports and documents, looking for something that was missed. And you found Brandon. That may be the key we've been hoping for. The only thing I've managed to do is find a connection. And I did that by searching somewhere that I suspect no one has thought to look." She saw the expression on my face, and continued, apparently still regretting her comments. "I'd guess there have been way more than a hundred well-qualified detectives, investigators, lab people, crime scene techs and the like working on this case over the past few years, not to mention the outside consultants, like the forensic DNA lab. But no one's come up with what they've been looking for—a link to a likely suspect. And so, what do you do when everything else has failed? You go in a different direction; you try something new. That's where we are now, I think, and this may be nothing, but it's worth pursuing, I believe."

"Lauren, please don't apologize," I said. "I'm amazed that we're—no, you're—making progress, and I want to hear about it, so tell me, please."

"Mr. O'Toole, in this business, you learn pretty quickly that everything is a team effort. We're all on the same team." She reached over and picked up one of the books; it was another yearbook. "The four yearbooks I brought in yesterday were from Vidalia High School. But the city school system there has four separate schools in all, a primary, an elementary, and a middle school. The J. R. Trippe Middle School is the site of the sixth, seventh and eighth grades, after which students move on to the city high school. This yearbook," Lauren said, "is from the Trippe Middle School the same year that Peter Davis and Brandon Wiggins were seniors at Vidalia High. Let me show you a couple of class members."

Flipping to the eighth-grade photos, she pointed to an image of Mary Nelle Davis, a much younger Mindy. "And look at this one," she said, pointing to a cute girl with long, dark hair. The caption under the photo read "Carole Marie Hastings."

"Who is that?" I asked.

"Carole Marie Hastings is now the Mrs. Peter Davis, Jr. Mindy's brother married her classmate."

"How and where did you discover that?"

"One of the online newspaper archive sites. Keyword search looking for Peter's wedding announcement. Carole and Mindy are both about the same age, between four and five years behind Peter. They were in the eighth grade when he was a senior in high school. When you're that age the difference is like a canyon, but once you get in your twenties, dating some guy four or five years older is not a big deal. Carole ended up going to the University of Georgia. I'm not sure if she overlapped with Peter there, but some way or another they got engaged and then married during his last year of medical school."

"Okay, so how does this tie in with Brandon?" I asked.

"He and Carole were at UGA at the same time. I called the sheriff of Toombs County. They did the investigation when Brandon went missing and was assumed to have drowned in the river. I was really just looking for background but as it turned out, the sheriff knew the situation well. He owns a bit of timberland and before he went missing, Wiggins had been his forester. He told me Brandon took a couple of years off between his sophomore and junior years to work with a forester there in Vidalia to be sure that was the career he wanted. So, when he started back at UGA, he would have been a junior when Carole was a freshman. The sheriff said they were pretty serious, but then Carole and Peter Davis started dating and, to quote what he told me, 'She wanted to marry the doctor.' Brandon married someone else a few years later.

I wasn't sure how this fit in. "According to the sheriff, he suspects Brandon was seeing Mindy," Lauren said.

That was a shock. "My god, if that was even a possibility, why the hell didn't he call and let somebody know?"

"There was basically no reason to do so at the time. We didn't know then what we know now. From his perspective, Brandon appeared to have died in a fishing accident. It happens all the time, and the evidence suggested that. Mindy lived and worked in Savannah. He knew her and her family of course, and he was aware of—how did he put it?—'her lifestyle.' And it really wasn't clear exactly when she went missing."

"But how…?" I began.

"I know what you're going to ask and I was getting to that. The sheriff knew Brandon and his wife were having problems. Brandon did some work for him, and I guess you could describe them as friends. He mentioned to the sheriff that he and his wife had talked about divorce and had sort of worked things out for the time being, but wasn't sure how long they would stay together. The other thing he said was that Brandon—and I'll quote this exactly, too—'couldn't keep his pants zipped,' and was running around on the wife. In fact, that may have been the problem in the first place."

"But Mindy…?"

"Just let me get to that part. You've got to put this in context. The sheriff said that several years ago—he couldn't remember the exact date, but it was a good while before Mindy went missing—he was on a routine patrol late one afternoon up north of Vidalia. He was driving down the dirt road that ran by the farm that belonged to the Davis family. He knew that no one was supposed to be living in the house, but noticed that there was a car and a pickup parked out front. So, just to be sure all was well, he turned in and drove up the drive. Before he could get out of his car even, Mindy comes out to see what was going on. He knew her family and recognized her immediately. He said he was just checking to be sure everything was okay. She thanked him and reminded him that she now owned the house with her brother who was off in school. She was just doing some housekeeping or something like that. Well, that would have been fine, except that he recognized the pickup as Brandon's truck. He sort of politely asked if she had company, and Mindy sort of looked a little embarrassed and said, 'Yes,' so the sheriff said, 'Y'all be real careful, hear,' and got on his way. He told me he had never mentioned that to anyone until I spoke with him earlier today."

CHAPTER 30

I was stunned. Mindy had many male "friends" for sure, but if she were truly having an affair with Brandon, this could change the whole picture. She had known him for years—presumably since grade school—making it likely that their relationship was more than casual. In that case, Brandon's disappearance and presumed death were not necessarily accidental. If his wife knew, or found out, her anger might have become a motive for harming not only her husband, but also Mindy, the object of his desire. But with his body never found, no one really knew what became of him. Could he and Mindy have gotten in a dispute? Perhaps he was drinking and things got physical? Mindy is accidentally killed, so he disposes of her body and then fakes his own death and disappears to start life anew elsewhere? The more I thought about the possible iterations, the more confused I became, and with that, all the less confident that the murderer would ever be found. Laying in my bed that night, I tossed and turned for what seemed like hours before I finally drifted off to sleep.

At ten the next morning, the four of us, Pete, Jack, Lauren and me, assembled in the conference room to discuss the case. Trying to read everyone's attitude as we chatted before getting down to business, Pete seemed skeptical, Jack hopeful, and Lauren confident. I wasn't sure how I felt. I took the lead, giving Lauren credit for her assistance and going over what we had and had not learned about the case. The one finding that seemed to have promise was the discovery of Brandon Wiggins's name, the fact that he disappeared on the same weekend as Mindy, and the hint that the two of them might have been romantically involved. Lauren did most of the talking; I commented when it seemed appropriate, mentioning that Jenna and I had driven up to look at the Davis farmhouse, and the call I received from Peter Davis afterwards. Pete and Jack sat quietly, listening and scribbling notes. She finished with details of what she had learned from the Toombs County sheriff. Breaking the momentary silence that followed, Pete said, "Damn!" Jack said, "Amazing!" I was quiet. Lauren glowed.

"You know this changes everything," Pete said. "I worked on this case, as did a lot of other people on the force, but if this turns out to lead somewhere, it may be a real break."

Jack sat silently thinking for a moment, then said, "Yes, but how did Wiggins's name get on the list of those to be interviewed, and where did the 'boyfriend' with a question mark label come from?" After another moment of silence, he continued, "Have you checked the tip hot line or the 911 register?"

"You think…?" Pete said, sitting up. Turning toward Lauren and me, he continued, "Have either of you two seen any records of tips that might have been called in, or anything like that? After the Davis girl went missing, we posted a few notices in the paper urging anyone who had any knowledge of the case to call our twenty-four hour hotline. It's managed at the same site as the 911 call center, but is monitored by a different group of operators. Those records are recorded and permanently maintained, and most of them have the phone number of the caller. That could be…"

"I thought calls to the tip hotline were confidential," I interrupted.

"Well, yes and no. The 911 lines are reserved for emergencies. The name and address of the caller pops up on the screen—presuming it's not blocked or faked—and that becomes a part of the record in case there's legal or law enforcement involvement. On the other hand, anyone who calls the tip line is told that what they say or allege is 'held confidential,' but that's kind of a play on words. We usually know who they are and the number they're calling from, but it would probably take a court order to act on the information and even then I suspect that anything that came out of it wouldn't be admissible in court. If a tip about a specific case comes in, the operator writes it up and passes it on to the correct agency."

"When you say 'writes it up and passes it on,' does that mean emailed, or sent as a text or what?" I asked.

Jack Garrett answered the question. "On a practical basis, they pick up the phone and call. Theoretically, they make a written notation of some sort for the files, but if one or more of the operators is out sick, or it's a particularly busy night, that may not get done. But that's not to say there's no record of the call or what was said, it's just that sometimes it's hard to document how they followed up with it."

Lauren spoke this time. "So what we've got to do is search the 911 and hotline files around the time notices were put in the paper, or on TV, or online?"

"Yep," Pete and Jack both replied simultaneously.

"That's kind of my thing." Lauren said. "I'll get on it right away, but I'm not familiar with the system, and I've got to do some research on the notices first. I'm not sure how long it will take."

We took a break for a few minutes, walking down the hall to grab coffee or drinks from the vending machines. Back in the conference room I said to Pete and Jack, "We know with some certainty how Mindy was killed, and it's possible that following up on a call to the hotline may point to a suspect, but we still don't know where the murder occurred. We have no crime scene. But, assuming the Toombs sheriff was correct when he saw her and recognized Brandon's truck at the farm house, could that be a possibility? Could we send in a crime scene crew to go over it in detail? I know it's been several years, but...."

"No way," Pete answered, "but it's a good suggestion. The same thought crossed my mind when Lauren was talking about it earlier. About the only way we could legitimately search that house would be if the legal owner—Mindy's brother—agreed in advance. And after what he said to you when he found out you'd been there, I don't think there's a snowball's chance in hell of that happening."

"Yes, but we know Mindy was frequently there and we have a witness who saw Brandon's truck there. Both Mindy and Brandon disappeared at the same time, more or less, and...."

"You're exactly correct," Pete said with a kind smile. "We'd term that 'reasonable suspicion.' But the Fourth Amendment specifically states that a search of someone's home or possessions cannot be made unless there is 'probable cause' that a crime has been or is going to be committed. The same standard applies to arrests. Except in emergencies, both require a warrant issued in advance. If we somehow managed to talk a judge into issuing a warrant to search that farmhouse based on what we know now, and then found everything we needed to identify Mindy's killer, that evidence would be inadmissible, and any case based on it thrown out of court."

Embarrassed at having made the suggestion, I replied, "Okay," justifying my stupidity by reminding myself that once upon a time my legal practice had been limited to environmental law. Hoping to redeem myself I said, "Let me throw out another suggestion then, something that occurred to me last night as I was trying to drift off to sleep. We don't know if Brandon Wiggins's disappearance had anything at all to do with Mindy's murder, but we can't ignore that there was some connection there, particularly the fact that they both disappeared on the same weekend. Her body was found, but his wasn't. It's not unreasonable to suggest that he accidently drowned, but it's an assumption, or better a 'reasonable suspicion' based on what he told his wife and where his truck was found." I nodded at Pete who was listening intently. "My understanding is that Mindy's body was discovered totally by fortune. Someone stumbled on the scene. No one was looking there or had reason to do so. What if Brandon was murdered at the same time as Mindy and his body hidden—presumably buried—in the same general area? The crime scene techs focused on the recovery of one set of remains. I'm sure they surveyed the area, but it had been several years since Mindy's murder, and if there were another hidden grave nearby, it could easily have been missed."

"That's a very interesting theory," Jack Garrett spoke up. "What are you proposing?"

"A search of the Davis farmhouse would be the search for a crime scene based on the speculation that a killing occurred there and the body disposed of elsewhere. I understand why that's not possible. But what if two people were killed and someone needed to hide two bodies? They'd pick out a place where they were reasonably certain no one would look and hide them both there. I doubt if the Bulloch County landowner would object to another search in the same general area where Mindy's remains were found. And in that case, 'probable cause' would not be an issue."

CHAPTER 31

For a few seconds, the table was silent, then everyone seemed to speak at once. "That's a damned good idea," Pete said. "We might just find something that will blow this whole thing open," Jack said, his tone one of eagerness. "Nice!" Lauren observed, her arms crossed over her chest. It took only a few minutes of discussion to come up with a tentative set of plans. All agreed that even if the search turned up nothing, we would have made progress in the sense that we excluded one possibility.

"We'll need to get the GBI involved," Pete said. "The site is in rural Bulloch County, and of course we have to have the blessing and cooperation of the sheriff up there. I worked on the case when it was active, and I think I know who to call at both agencies to get the ball rolling on this. I'm not sure about the landowner, though. I'll ask the local guys to handle getting something in writing from him. And just to be sure, I can't see any problem in getting the local magistrate judge to give us a search warrant. We do not want to screw this up." We decided to check in with each other the first of the next week. Lauren said she would try to have something to report on the possibility of a tip line or 911 call.

The next day being Friday, for a change I was in my office at the gallery when Jessica arrived for work. "What are you doing here?" she asked. "I thought you were off doing your Sherlock Holmes stuff."

"Hey, give me a break, please. I got involved because it's something that meant a lot to Jenna." Jessica frowned. "And she means a lot to me...."

"Okay…." she said, and went back to her desk at the front of the gallery. Was she jealous?

I called Jenna and arranged a date for Saturday night, then spent the rest of the day catching up on emails, bills and all the things I should have been doing otherwise. Working on Mindy's case was taking a toll on both my business and my relationships. As much as I wanted to believe good art would sell itself, the gallery couldn't run on autopilot. Jessica and Hattie needed my presence and support. And with Jenna, discussing Mindy or just about anything to do with her death, was akin to reopening an old wound that instead should be given time to heal.

The weekend provided a much needed break. Having spent what were now countless hours surrounded by the blank walls of the conference room in Savannah, Jenna and I drove up the coast to Beaufort, South Carolina, spent the night in a small inn a few blocks from the waterfront, ate fresh seafood washed down with decent wine, and generally ignored the rest of the world. Mindy's name was not mentioned.

By Monday, I felt refreshed and was looking forward to seeing what progress Pete and Lauren had made over the weekend. Pete called to check in, saying he had gotten the verbal permission of the landowner to search further at the site where Mindy's remains were found. He was arranging to get that in a signed document. He spoke with the Bulloch County sheriff and was offered their assistance. A call to the magistrate judge there confirmed that getting a formal search warrant for the property would be no problem. Pete's contact at the GBI was less certain. He implied that the idea sounded like "a fishing expedition," and that "it would require significant time and resources" to get the team from the Coastal Crime Lab in

Savannah "over there without more evidence" and a well-defined location to search. He suggested the low-budget option of having a cadaver dog search the site, and if the dog alerted on a certain area, calling in a team with ground-penetrating radar to confirm a possible burial. "Sounds like the guy is worried about his budget," Pete observed.

"So, what do you want to do?" I asked.

"The dog and his trainer will be there the day after tomorrow. I could have gotten him earlier, but I want to get the paperwork—the permission and the warrant—done first."

"You're on top of this," I said.

"It's been a cold case for too long. And this was your idea. You want to be there?," Pete asked.

"I'd like to, but I need to do some catching up here at my business. I'm not sure what I could add anyway."

"Okay, I'll call and let you know what we find."

I had not been off the phone with Pete for more than ten minutes when Lauren called. She began with, "These people are so disorganized...," going on to explain how if she were running things at the call center "they would be very, very different—and far more efficient." Her main complaint seemed to be that there was no organized way to search the calls coming in to either 911 or to the police tip line. "There are records to be sure, but if I were in charge, each would be classified under about a dozen basic criteria and entered into a searchable database...."

"Hold on," I said, stopping her mid-sentence. "I'm sure there are organizational problems, but tell me what you found."

"At this point, very little. I'm approaching this backwards. Rather than look for something specific in the subject of a call,

I'm excluding other things that I'm not looking for, so what is left may tell me what I want to know."

I wasn't sure if I understood what she was trying to say, but told her that sounded like a smart move.

"Thank you," Lauren said. "I am planning to finish this up in three more days. I'll call you."

I worked at the gallery for the next two days, taking off early on Wednesday afternoon to run some errands and do some grocery shopping. It was nearly six by the time I returned to my apartment. I was just putting up the groceries when my cell rang; it was Pete Marsh, nearly yelling into the phone. "Oh, boy, John, you really missed it!"

"Missed what?"

"The dog, a beautiful German Shepherd named 'Radar.' It was the most amazing performance I think I've ever seen...."

"What...?"

"Let me tell you. The trainer—his name is Freddy—has been working with this dog for about five years. He gets calls from all over the state. The dog is trained for cadaver work, but has also helped out with collapsed buildings and that sort of thing. Well, we started out where the crime lab had exhumed Mindy's bones. He—the dog, not Freddy—sniffed there and barked and sat down. Freddy said that confirmed there'd been a body there at one time. So we had sort of laid out a grid and he starts searching, sniffing back and forth, wagging his tail and just really into what he was doing. And then, about thirty or thirty-five feet up—that's north—of where Mindy's remains were found, right on the edge of the hedgerow but a little out in the hayfield, Radar stops and begins sniffing and pawing at the earth there, then he begins barking, almost howling, really, and sits down. Freddy said that was a hit—a strong hit. Something, someone, is buried there."

"Amazing," I said, not fully knowing how to react. "What happens next? Are the crime scene techs coming out?"

"I hope. I called my GBI contact. He said something to the effect that many times these things were false alerts. Maybe somebody shot a deer, took the good cuts of meat and buried the rest. Or an animal died there. He wants to send out the GPR people before…."

"GPR?"

"Sorry, ground-penetrating radar. He said he needed a confirmation by that method before sending out the crime scene team. He mentioned something again about what it costs…. The bastard!"

"That's great, I think. When are the GPR folks coming?"

"Day-after-tomorrow, Friday. They're a private firm that specialize in that. Most of what they do is work for private and municipal cemeteries, especially the old ones. Don't want to be digging a grave and find out somebody's already claimed the spot. But the good thing, I hope, is that they should know right away if something is there. If we get a hit, I was promised the guys from the Crime Lab will be here Monday morning." Pete stopped to take a deep breath. "If things work out confirmation-wise and we get that far, do you want to be here with the crime scene crew?"

"I think so. I'll keep Monday open just in case."

CHAPTER 32

As promised, Lauren called on Thursday just before noon. I respected her for her abilities and I liked her personally. She was obviously very intelligent, and appeared to be quite talented in her field of information technology. But the more I knew her, the more I came to believe that a touch of OCD was one of the basic requirements for an entry-level position in that discipline. "Finally," she began, "I've been making some progress. If you want to hear the truth, I used to think that people called 911 for emergencies, and police tip lines to help solve crimes. But no, it's almost anything else.... They call 911 because the neighbor's dog is barking too loud, or somebody's baby-daddy won't pay attention to the baby-mama and they want the cops to go by his house and talk to him, that kind of thing. And it appears the tip line attracts all sorts of weirdos, people who seriously believe in alien abductions, or know of a good psychic who can help solve crimes by summoning up the spirits of the dead. But I did manage to figure out how to sift my way through the list of calls received in response to the requests put out in the media after Mindy's disappearance. It was no easy task. This happened years ago, and the file box was stuffed away in some storage room and then I had to link that to the recordings which were stored on a massive set of ancient and very slow servers...." She stopped realizing she was getting off track.

"There were a total of fifty-one responses. Of those, about forty were not helpful in any way. There were a number of nut cases who rambled on about this or that, several people who said they thought they had seen Mindy or someone who resembled her at various places like the mall, or Hardee's or at a car dealership in Pooler, those kind of things. Three women left word that they knew what kind of woman she was, working as a stripper in that club, and that she had been 'smitten by the Lord' or gone into hiding. One man spoke about hearing about a distant cousin of Ted Bundy who had become a serial killer of young women on the East Coast and thought she might be one of his victims. But I did find a recording of one person suggesting that Brandon Wiggins was Mindy's 'boyfriend' and might be a suspect in her disappearance. I listened to it several times to be sure I wasn't missing anything, and wrote it down verbatim. I'll read it to you in a minute...."

"That's wonderful," I said. "Did they leave their name, or a number to call for follow up or anything like that?"

"I'm getting to that, and to answer your question, no, they didn't leave any contact information, but the system made a record of the time and phone number so we know when, and where the person was located when they called. It was from a branch of the public library on Johnny Mercer Boulevard, just off US-80 between downtown Savannah and the Islands Expressway and just after two in the afternoon. The voice was female, but I couldn't say much about it beyond that. Here's what she said:

> Hello, I saw the piece in the *Morning News* asking for the public's help in finding Mary Nelle Davis—the paper said her nickname was "Mindy"—because she has been missing for about two weeks and no one has seen her. Well, I will have to say I don't know her personally, but I do know for a fact that she has been sneaking around and seeing a married man, his name is Brandon Wiggins and he lives in Vidalia, Georgia. He has the

reputation of being a philanderer and ignores his wife, instead preying on the wives of other men and wrecking their marriages and bringing disgrace to their families. He's apparently been seeing this Mary Nelle woman, who works in a sex club in Savannah and told someone who knows him that they are boyfriend and girlfriend, but they are certainly old enough to know better. And he drinks to excess, too, and may be taking drugs. I have been told all this from a very accurate source who knows the situation. I would talk to him and find out what he knows.

That's it," Lauren said. "What do you think?"

"I honestly don't know. It would be good to hear the actual recording. I'd like to hear the tone of her voice, the inflection and emphasis and the like."

"I agree, and if the call center had up-to-date equipment, I'd have that for you. I brought a flash drive for the purpose of getting a copy, but I was told it wasn't that simple and that their IT people would have to download it for me. I'll let you know when I have it."

The recording Lauren had found was interesting and perhaps revealing in the sense that more than one person knew about Mindy's relationship to Brandon. But it didn't seem to move us any closer to understanding who killed her or why she was killed. The wild card at this point was Brandon. If the assumed facts—he drowned in an accident—were correct, that was one thing. If the "hit" by the cadaver dog near Mindy's burial site revealed something else, a lot of theories would need to be reconsidered. I was eager to hear what the GPR crew would find.

I woke up early Friday morning, thinking this would be an important day. I worked at the gallery, but all through the morning I found myself nervously glancing at my phone, thinking I might have missed a call or text, but at the same time knowing I had not. By 2:00 p.m. Pete Marsh had not called. I picked up the phone to call him, but thinking better of it, laid it back on my desk.

The call came at 3:23 p.m., five minutes after Jessica had asked me why I was pacing about so much. "Hey, John," Pete said. "We're good to go. The GPR people's equipment lit up like a Christmas tree when they scanned the area that the dog focused on. I've been on the phone with the Crime Lab. They will be here Monday morning at 10:00 a.m., assuming the weather holds. They can't do a good job of examining the site if it's raining. Can you be here?" Could I not be there I asked myself, telling Pete I'd arrive early. He said he'd text me exact directions about finding the site.

"I want to hear some details. Tell me what you know, please."

"You've sort of got to see it to understand it, but the instrument they use is relatively small. It looks a bit like a push-type lawnmower, a little flat-decked platform mounted on wheels that the operator slowly rolls back and forth over the area he's scanning. Up on the handle, there's a small flat screen—looks like an iPad, really—and that's his readout. It's a sort of sonar arrangement—the bottom deck thing sends out what they call 'electromagnetic pulses' into the earth, and they are reflected off what's in the ground, bounce back and show up as a pattern on the screen. Like I said, you've got to see it to understand it better. But the bottom line is this: in an area that measures roughly two feet wide by six feet long, the soil has been disturbed down to about forty-five inches, a little less than four feet. Near the bottom of that space there is a large object with variable echoes that the operator guy says is compatible with a buried body. They won't know that for sure, or anything else until someone does some digging. And next to the object they think is a body is an area of really intense echoes. The guy was focusing on that. He's not sure what it is, but it appears to be solid—metal maybe, like a big belt buckle or tin can or something like that. He just couldn't say. Several Bulloch County deputies have been here ever since we got started this morning. They're going to post a guard over the weekend to make sure no one disturbs anything."

"So we'll know something on Monday for sure, you think?" I asked.

"I think we'll have some idea of the direction this investigation will take. That's about all I can say. Think about it. Mindy went missing. Years later her body is discovered, yet we're still no closer to finding her killer than we were when she disappeared. Yes, this may be another body. It may well be Brandon's. But the question to be answered is this: Will that finding move us any closer to discovering who is responsible for their deaths?"

CHAPTER 33

I spent the weekend in Savannah. Normally, I would have been with Jenna, but she was off for a "girls' weekend" with friends in the mountains. As much as I enjoyed her company, it turned out to be for the best. I had not mentioned anything to her about the preliminary findings at Mindy's burial site, but my anxiety and nervous anticipation would have been hard to hide. I tried to relax, read a book, take a stroll in the neighborhood, or anything else to pass the time. I obsessed about what might be found, running various situations and "what ifs" through my mind. Jenna called late Sunday afternoon to let me know she was back. I did my best to sound nonchalant and relaxed. We talked about getting together midweek, and once again, Mindy's name was never mentioned.

I was awake and up before 6:00 a.m. on Monday, pacing about and wondering in a weird way what one wears to watch the exhumation of a murder victim. I decided on blue jeans and boots, with a nondescript work shirt and a light jacket. I programmed the address Pete had texted into Google Maps. Most of the route was on I-16 West, arriving at the site in forty-seven minutes, more or less. I wanted to be there early, so I left at 8:30, following the interstate to the Statesboro exit, then navigating a series of progressively smaller paved roads until I saw a field entrance marked with red and blue flagging tape and leading to an irregularly parked group of vehicles half-hidden behind a bushy hedgerow. Pete Marsh saw me coming and pointed where to park. "Gotta keep the road open for the crime lab crew," he yelled.

About fifteen minutes later a short caravan of cars and vans pulled in the field and drove up. The local sheriff and several deputies, accompanied by Pete, met them and gave a quick guided tour of the site. I tagged along, introduced to the group only as "an investigator for the Savannah police." In the several months since Mindy's remains were recovered, the weather had smoothed the disturbed soil and a fresh crop of grass and weeds had taken over the small mounds of earth. The new site, about two car-lengths away, was bounded by long metal stakes at each corner and declared off-limits by a long cordon of yellow "Crime Scene" tape. A paunchy, middle-aged man, whom Pete identified as the "GPR guy" consulted with an intense-looking woman from the crime lab. "She's the boss," Pete half-whispered in a low voice. After an initial walk-through, the yellow tape was removed, and techs began making measurements and taking photographs. A stenographer of sorts followed them around, making notes on a clipboard-mounted legal pad. Within half an hour a tent, roughly twenty feet on each side, had been erected over the possible gravesite and the excavation begun.

The random grass and weeds were carefully removed and passed on to two men standing next to a couple of sieves, which appeared to be made of window screen mounted in a wooden frame and supported by folding sawhorses. Every bit of dirt, plant material and debris removed from or near the burial site was sifted through the sieves, the two men searching for anything of importance. The photographer stood nearby, taking dozens of photos as the opening grew larger. While all this was taking place, Pete and I, together with a dozen or more deputies and crime lab staff stood on the sidelines, watching intently.

After nearly an hour, one of the trowel-wielding excavators called out, "Got something." I maneuvered around so as to catch a glimpse of a dark black irregular object at one end of the hole. Everything else stopped as the team focused on the area and the camera person hovered and snapped photos. A few minutes later, a bulky but well-preserved black plastic trash bag was lifted out of the hole, photographed and passed on to two gloved techs for preliminary examination.

"They'll make a quick initial survey, then put whatever they have in a sealed container to take back to the lab for analysis, fingerprint ID, that kind of stuff...." Pete explained.

I watched intently from a distance. The black bag appeared to have been twisted, looped over and tied at the top. One of the techs, a middle-aged woman, gingerly teased the knot apart, spread the top and peered into the bag. She first removed something made of blue cloth—a pair of blue jeans—then a shirt and a pair of men's boots. All were passed over to be photographed. I could see from the way the bag sagged that there was still something heavy in the bottom. Spreading the top open a bit further, the tech reached in and extracted a what appeared to be a stainless steel revolver. I wasn't sure because of the distance, but it looked to be about the size of a .38 caliber. Reaching in again, she pulled out a black automatic pistol with the distinctive silhouette of a .40 caliber Glock. She laid both pistols side by side on the table as the photographer bent over them, snapping images.

"Damn!" Pete muttered, speaking more to himself than to me. "That sure complicated things." Turning to me, he said, "You know, you can be damned sure that whoever buried that stuff wrapped up in a garbage bag didn't expect it to ever be found."

"Why's that?" I asked, not sure what he meant.

"Preserved the evidence. If it were buried in the dirt, pretty soon mother nature would have gone a long ways toward helping things rot, or rust or whatever. Not so much now, though. I'll be so very interested to hear what the lab folks come up with once they get it all back to Savannah."

Everyone took a break for lunch. Just before noon, a patrol car from the Bulloch County Sheriff's Department arrived with a large haul of hamburgers, barbecue sandwiches, chips, iced tea, soft drinks and the like, laying them out buffet fashion on the tailgates of several pickups. We ate standing up in the shade of the hedgerow. Around one o'clock, the excavation resumed. As the techs got closer to the bottom, a vague stench of rotting meat could be detected. The observers, the deputies, other crime lab personnel, and Pete and I backed away a bit. By two o'clock the head crime lab person announced that they were about to lift "something" out of the pit and suggested we all stay a good distance away. We complied, and the crowd reassembled itself back near the parked vehicles.

The techs, now all dressed in white disposable jumpsuits and wearing masks, gloves and hair coverings, erected two broad-based supports on each side of the hole, then from a connecting crosspiece created pairs, from which they suspended a chain hoist rig extending into the pit. Momentarily, the techs who had been working inside the pit climbed out, and began to winch up a large object resting in a sling suspended from the hoists. From our perspective, the object also appeared to have been wrapped in black plastic garbage bags. The stench of death was immediately overwhelming. The crowd of observers backed away even further.

Two other techs, also dressed in protective gear and carrying a long stretcher, approached the pit from one side. They stood at each end and eased the stretcher next to the object suspended over the excavation. The first two techs, now standing in the pit, attempted to transfer the black-wrapped object from the hoist's sling onto the stretcher. In the middle of the transfer, a wall of the pit next to one of the supports suddenly crumbled, caving into the pit and dropping one end of the suspended object toward the stretcher. One of the techs reflexly reached out, attempting to keep it in place but in the process grabbing hold of the plastic bag that covered one end. We all watched in horror as the bag slid off to reveal the blackened and shriveled face of the corpse that once was Brandon Wiggins.

CHAPTER 34

The crowd of observers, at least those of us who had a direct view of what happened, responded with a spontaneous collective gasp and a primal urge to flee the ghoulish sight. Murmurs and exclamations of "No!" and "Oh, my god," and "What is that?" and similar blended into a cacophony of horror and disgust. As one, we backed even further away from the exhumation, scattering into small groups in the surrounding hayfield. Even Pete Marsh, the veteran homicide detective, hustled over to the hedgerow and vomited violently. Wiping his face with his handkerchief as he returned, he apologized with, "Well, I was not expecting that." My physical and mental reactions were less visible, but no less shocking; over the years I have learned the art of concealing them.

"I would presume this raises more questions than it answers," I said.

"To be sure," Pete replied. "This case is ours now though, and we need to meet as soon as possible to plan some strategy. The first thing the crime lab will do is try to identify that body. I'd give you hundred-to-one odds it's Wiggins, and that's going to shape the direction of things from here on out. And the pistols. Nobody would dump them like that if they didn't have something to do with the crime. We know enough now to start planning, but if this case is like others I've had dealings with, the crime lab will release information in dribs and drabs, and a full final report will take months. Trouble is, the longer the delay, the greater the chance that the murderer will abscond, or try to hide more potential evidence, or even attempt to silence any potential witnesses that might testify against him...."

"Or her," I added.

"You're correct—the old 'heaven has no rage' thing." Marsh looked about, then glanced at his watch. "I need to get back to Savannah. I'll speak to the crew here and thank everyone for their help, then I'll be on the road. I'll find out when the crime lab techs think they'll be finished here and let you know. And I need to call Jack Garrett. He's one of the best, and I surely would like to have his thoughts and input." We were both soon on I-16 headed back to Savannah.

It had been a strange and unsettling few hours. This case, Mindy's death and now what appeared to be the murder of her lover had, in one form or another, dominated my life since that disaster of a day at the Prado in Madrid, months earlier. Like an insidious virus, it infected almost everything I cared about, from Jenna, to my work, to my sense of well-being. And now, just perhaps, the end was in sight. But would this be a grand finale or the whimpering close to a disturbing and foul series of events? I did not know, and that in itself was a further cause of anxiety.

I arrived back at the gallery mid-afternoon and spent the rest of the day hiding in my office with the door shut, mostly playing Sudoku on my cell phone. I told Jessica I wanted to review some marketing proposals I'd received, but I believe she knew better. Pete Marsh called just before five. He'd arranged a meeting at police headquarters the following day at four. I said I'd be there. "This has turned into an active case again, and your interest in it is a hundred percent of the reason. I know everyone is grateful, but I hope you don't mind if I take charge at this point. I still want you to be part of things. You're a sworn investigator for the department, so there's no problem with that." I said that would be fine; the ball would be in someone else's court from now until things were wrapped up. I took a deep breath of relief.

We met once more at the Habersham Street headquarters, but this time in a larger conference room with windows looking out on the live oak trees growing in the park-like median of Oglethorpe Avenue. Again, it was the four of us, Pete Marsh, Jack Garrett, Lauren Yates and me. Pete had been on the phone with the crime lab and gave us an update. "It's far too soon to get any details, but I've learned enough to get us started. First, even though the DNA confirmation has not been completed, everyone is certain that the body is that of Brandon Wiggins. Now this is the interesting part. The first garbage bag they pulled out of the hole there had his clothes in it, and that included his wallet with Brandon's IDs. The body itself—like Mindy's—was naked." Pete suppressed a smirk, saying, "You can make what you will of that," then continued, "The first thing the lab often does when they get a case like this is run the body through a CT scanner. That appeared to give us the cause of his death. There were two slugs in his chest cavity; they'll know more about that when the autopsy is completed. From an investigation perspective, the good thing about this—if you can say there's anything good about a violent crime—is that whoever killed and buried him put the body in two oversized heavy-duty plastic bags, the kind you might put yard debris in. Brandon would have been bleeding heavily if he'd been shot in the chest, so the supposition is that they bagged him to keep from spilling blood everywhere when they moved the body to bury it. That's speculation, of course, but it was a stupid move in the sense that the body is amazingly well preserved, mummified really, after being in the ground for several years. And I guess they threw his clothes and the pistols in the other bag just to have a way to carry them out. Any questions thus far?"

The rest of us sat quietly. "I'm sure we'll have some," Jack said, "but go ahead with what else you've found out."

"That's really about it so far. The lab's only had the body for less than twenty-four hours, and I am sure there's lots more that we'll learn. We now have a second victim buried next to the first. We know there was a connection there, and are assuming they were killed and buried at the same time…."

"Is 'connection' the correct word?" Lauren asked. I wasn't sure if she was being serious.

"Whatever…." Pete replied with a straight face, then continued. "First off, we need to define two things: where we think the murders occurred, and who would have reason and opportunity to kill these two. Could I suggest we think about this and other priorities and meet back here later in the week? I asked the lab about the pistols and hoped to have something to tell you today, but they're still working on it. They should have something by, say, Friday. Is that a good time for everyone to talk? We can do a video conference call if that would be easier."

Jack raised his hand. "I'm the old farmer these days. I haven't gotten updated in the world of technology. Reckon we could meet in person?"

Lauren spoke up. "I agree." Pete looked at me. I nodded.

"Okay, we'll meet here Friday at 2:00 p.m. Please write down your questions, make and bring your lists, and come back with some thoughts on where we should go next."

Back at my apartment, I sat down with a legal pad, trying to decide how I should approach making a list. At the top of one page I wrote "Mindy" and on a second page "Brandon." Below, I divided each page into two columns, the first labeled

"Name" and the second "Motive." To be a suspect, I reasoned that a person's name had to appear on both pages, and along with it, a serious reason to consider doing harm to Mindy, or Brandon, or both. While a deep simmering dislike was what I initially had in mind, I reasoned I also needed to consider a sudden bout of unrestrained anger, for example, Brandon's wife surprising him in bed with another woman. From what we knew thus far, it appeared that the bodies of both were naked at the time of their burial. In consideration of that, I added a third column labeled "Heat of the Moment." Laying both pages in front of me on my desk, I tried to think about who would meet the criteria I set out.

First, there was Brandon's wife, Anna. I knew nothing of her, but Lauren had heard they were having marital problems. If she knew about Mindy, or thought of her as "the other woman," that would be reason enough. And if she surprised them *in flagrante*, that would qualify for the anger column. I put her name on both lists.

Then there was Peter, Mindy's brother. Two people said they saw them arguing in front of the farmhouse, accompanied by yelling and shoving. My tendency was to discount that. Besides, when Mindy disappeared, Peter was living in Cleveland, Ohio, doing his cardiology training. On the other hand, I could think of half a dozen reasons he might be upset with Mindy, not the least of which was her lifestyle, and using the farm to host "parties." Peter was also a classmate of Brandon's, and appeared to have stolen his girlfriend. Brandon in turn seemed to be sleeping with Peter's sister while cheating on his wife. Plenty of things to cause anger. His name went on both lists.

Next was Carole, Peter's wife. I also knew nothing about her, but in the past she had a close relationship with Brandon before dumping him to marry Peter. Old flames often smolder. I knew of nothing to suggest they had been seeing each other prior to the murders, but still, in Carole's mind Mindy might qualify as competition for Brandon's affection. I added her name to the lists, but with a question mark each time.

And then there was Mrs. Davis, Mindy's mother. I thought about her a long time before adding her to the list under Mindy's and Brandon's names. Her attitude when I spoke with her was one of anger and resentment. She saw herself and her late husband as two honest, hard-working individuals who had raised themselves from near poverty through sacrifice and the sweat of their brows. Indeed, she was correct. But her daughter, despite the advantages and education she had been offered, had chosen a different path, that of "a common whore" in Mrs. Davis's own words. And if this were not enough, through her relationship with Brandon, Mindy was an adulteress, a flagrant violation of the Seventh Commandment. I added her name to both sheets.

Were there others? No doubt, but these four would have to be at the top of my list. I placed the sheets in a folder, intending to add to the roster as new candidates came to mind. What bothered me the most, however, was that Mindy, as beautiful and intelligent and talented as she might have been, didn't have to look far from home to find potential enemies.

CHAPTER 35

On Friday at 2:00 p.m. we were back in the same conference room at police headquarters. Each of us had brought a notebook or folder with their lists of potential suspects, possible crime scenes and other things that needed to be discussed. Pete started off by updating us on what he'd learned from the crime lab. "Lots of things are in the works, but the real bombshell is the story on the pistols. I wanted to call it a surprise, but the more I thought about it, the more I realized it was something we might have expected. As you may know, both pistols were buried in a plastic garbage bag with its top tied, so even though they've been in the ground for several years, there're in good shape. Soon after they got back to the lab, a tech ran the serial numbers and immediately got hits. Here are photos of each weapon," he said, passing out sheets with color images of the guns.

"The one at the top is a Model 642 hammerless stainless steel Smith & Wesson .38 revolver. It holds five rounds in the cylinder and is a pocket gun really, one with a low profile that you might carry for protection. The one at the bottom is a .40 caliber Glock Model 27. It is semiautomatic and can hold ten rounds, nine in the clip and one in the chamber. It's somewhat bigger than the revolver, but small enough to carried without a holster in one's pocket.

"The serial numbers on both pistols were clear, so tracking down the owners was not a problem. The revolver belonged to Brandon Wiggins. He purchased it about a year before his death. The Glock was purchased by Daniel Peter Davis, Jr. from a sporting goods store in Augusta in what would probably have been his final year of medical school. Now here's the interesting thing. About two weeks after Mindy went missing and as the search here in Savannah was just getting seriously started, Dr. Davis reported that someone had stolen that pistol out of his car. He was living in Cleveland, Ohio, at the time, so there was no reason to make a connection between the stolen gun and his sister's disappearance."

"Damn, Pete," Jack Garrett said, "that doesn't make the doctor look good."

"Well, maybe or maybe not. As far as we know, Peter was in Cleveland when all this happened. You could argue Mindy might have stolen the gun when her brother was home and he didn't notice it missing until he got back to Ohio. And remember those slugs in Brandon's chest? Once they recover them at autopsy, the lab can see if they match one of the two pistols. If they match Peter's gun, a good criminal defense attorney might make the argument that Brandon and Mindy got into a fight, she shot him, but he managed to choke her to death before he bled out." Pete paused then said in a facetious tone, "Of course, that would raise the question of who disposed of the bodies…." Only Lauren laughed. "But back to reality," he continued, "there are lots of situations we could imagine, but we need more information before we even start to speculate."

I spoke up. "I still think we need to search the farmhouse. If there were a bloody confrontation, wouldn't it be likely that there's still some evidence to be found there even though the killings happened several years ago?"

Pete grinned briefly, "You're getting ahead of me, John, but I agree. The problem is not what any one of us thinks though, it's convincing a judge to give us a search warrant that will stand up to scrutiny and appeals if something discovered during the search leads to anything—like murder charges. So, let's back up a bit and take this in an orderly fashion. We spoke the other day about making a list of individuals to focus on as possible suspects. I'd like to hear what each of you thinks, and I'll go last. Jack, you want to start?"

Jack fished in his shirt pocket to extract a pair of half-frame reading glasses that he propped on his nose, opened a folder and studied a written list before speaking. "Let me say first how I see these crimes happening. This was not a robbery, or a calculated hit, or anything planned in advance. This was a crime of passion—and I define that word broadly—and one that escalated as it evolved. It happened, it got out of hand, and those that were present—there had to be more than one—feared they'd be discovered. Mindy lived in Savannah, and the initial search was centered around that location. But I think from the conversations we've been having and from where the bodies were found, the killings took place elsewhere, probably in Toombs County. We need to look at whoever had an emotional connection with the victims. That includes both families. Somebody had to move Wiggins's truck, for example, and that someone would have to know where it could be discovered later and not raise suspicion. I'd rank Wiggins's wife—what's her name, Anna?—at the top of my list. But she didn't act alone. There are others involved. That's about all I have on that aspect." He took his glasses off, laid them on the table and waited for someone else to speak.

Pete looked at Lauren. "I'm not sure how much help I can be. I'm kinda the newbie here, but I agree with Detective Garrett. I think it's one or more of the women. Maybe I shouldn't speak from that viewpoint, but from what I've heard, the viciousness of this crime is astounding. And they all had some reason to be angry at either Mindy or Brandon or both of them. I'm thinking Brandon's wife, Anna, of course. Or Mindy's mother, or even Carole, the doctor's wife. Do you suppose that while her husband was working long hours at the hospital she was hooking up again with her college boyfriend? And how about Mindy's mother? From what John said, she acted like a real bitch, dissing her daughter and all. Of course, she'd be too old to do the killing herself…" Realizing her rhetoric was becoming somewhat heated, Lauren stopped suddenly, waiting for someone to comment. Jack nodded. Pete and I were silent.

"And you, John, who do you think we should be looking closely at?" Pete asked.

"I don't mean to sound like a broken record, but I have to agree with Jack and Lauren. There was a lot of emotion and violence that accompanied these killings. Mindy was severely beaten and strangled. Brandon was shot at least twice. At this point, I have to aim my suspicion at four people. I don't know any more than that. Jack mentioned Brandon's truck, so that one thing alone would imply that at least two people were involved. In no particular order, I would suspect Peter Davis, his mother, his wife Carole, and Brandon's wife, Anna. What do you think, Pete?"

"I don't have to say anything at all, because I believe we have all reached the same conclusions based on what we know now to be the same set of facts. In other words, my thinking is totally in line with that of you all. So, can I put that down as a consensus?" We all signified agreement.

"Okay, let's move on to the next thing," Pete continued. "John, twice now you've brought up searching the Davis family farmhouse in Toombs County as a possible crime scene. You've read and are up on the details of this investigation since day one. Pretend for a moment I'm a judge and you're a district attorney trying to get me to issue a search warrant. How would you handle it?"

Pete's request caught me unprepared, but better here than in a courtroom. "I think the answer to that question may depend on what the crime lab's findings turn out to be. But at the moment, I would stress that a horrific, violent double murder has been committed, crimes that reek of personal anger and vengeance. I would say those factors point at individuals with a personal relationship to the victims and that more than one person was involved. I would describe the victims as flawed individuals to be sure, but not deserving of their fates. Brandon Wiggins might be presented in the way the tip line caller referred to him, a philanderer with marital problems. And Mindy as a woman who had a future of wonderful potential, but fell into a lifestyle of disrepute which included an extramarital affair with Wiggins. A reliable witness, the Toombs County sheriff, was able to place Mindy and Brandon at the farmhouse north of Vidalia on one occasion. Mindy's car was found at her apartment, and Brandon's truck at a boat ramp on the Altamaha River. One or more persons had to have driven those vehicles to those locations, persons who knew both victims and knew where to park their vehicles so as not to immediately raise suspicion. So, in summary I would say to the judge that the murders involved more than one person, and were committed by those who knew the victims and their habits, and at a place familiar to all parties. At that point I would suggest the Davis family farmhouse, and request a warrant to conduct a forensic survey in search of evidence that a crime or crimes were committed there."

CHAPTER 36

"Sounds good," Pete said, "but we need more. I'm sure both Jack and I can tell you stories of cases—terrible crimes sometimes—that have been lost in court when the one or two pieces of evidence that were necessary to prove the case were tossed by a judge because of some error based on how law enforcement obtained them. Something you find that absolutely proves guilt becomes useless if you can't present it to a jury. The moment we commit to obtaining a search warrant is the moment we give up the lead in this investigation. The potential crime scenes and evidence sites are located in at least three counties and several cities, so with a multi-jurisdictional case like this the GBI will have to take a big role. We'll need to work with the district attorney for Toombs County to get a judge there to issue a warrant for the Davis farm, if that's what we want. So, before we back off and turn it over, I want to be sure we've gotten it right."

We talked at length, discussing what we might have neglected or anything more we should be doing before closing the door on this chapter. "You should be proud, John," Pete Marsh said. "In spite of whatever reservations you've had, it was you—your drive and curiosity—that kick-started this investigation once again, and possibly will lead to an indictment." He paused and then added, "Or indictments, plural."

It was not yet four o'clock when I left police headquarters and strolled back to the gallery. I was tired, mentally and physically. I checked in briefly with Jessica, and Hattie who was working on the accounts, then headed back to my apartment to take a nap. Now, just maybe, I could get on with my life.

Pete called on my cell just after sunset, waking me up from where I'd crashed on my sofa. "Hey, I've been on the phone ever since we finished up. I believe I've got things lined up. I'm going to formally take the lead for the Savannah/Chatham metro agency and will be honchoing things from here on until we make some arrests. The GBI will be assigning liaison people from Regions 5 and 12 to cover Bulloch, Toombs and Chatham Counties and anything in between. I need to get in touch with the district attorney for Toombs County to work out how he wants to handle getting a search warrant. There's lots to do. The main reason I called was to ask how involved you want to be in all this. You've put in a lot of time and energy. You want to step back completely and let us handle things, or do you want to stay in the loop?"

It was the kind of question I did not want to answer. Part of me said, "You've done your bit. That's enough," while another, more forceful voice insisted, "You can't bail now, just when you've almost seen this thing to its conclusion." I hesitated....

"You need to make up your mind, John. I suspect things are going to go rapidly from here on out," Pete said. "And no one's going to make any demands on you. I've gotten to know you well enough to realize you're not a quitter. So, what's it gonna be?"

"Okay, I'm in, but as an observer." Alarm bells were going off in my head.

"I thought you'd say that. It's addictive, isn't it?"

I thanked Pete and said goodbye without answering his question.

It was as if the merry-go-round had stopped spinning. For the next ten days or so, all was quiet. I woke up in the morning, spent the day at the gallery, saw Jenna either in Savannah or Claxton every several days and heard nothing from Pete Marsh, Jack Garrett or Lauren Yates. I told Jenna that the Mindy investigation was proceeding ahead, but had moved on to a phase that was beyond anything I could do. She asked only if I thought the murderer would be identified and caught, and seemed satisfied when I said, "I hope so." Brandon Wiggins was not discussed.

I was talking with a potential customer in the gallery on Friday afternoon of the following week when Pete called. I excused myself and stepped a few feet away to answer the call. "I want to give you an update. We're good to go on doing a search of the Davis farmhouse. It's taken a lot of talking and paperwork, but on Monday morning we'll have a search warrant which the GBI will serve on Dr. Davis as he arrives at his office at about 8:00 a.m. Meanwhile, the mobile crime scene lab will be on its way to Toombs County. I'll be right behind them. The sheriff and some of his deputies will meet us at the Vidalia exit off I-16 at about the same time and we'll go from there. I haven't seen the farmhouse firsthand, but we have the overall plans we pulled from the tax assessor's files. Do you want to go with me?"

"You know I do." I tried not to sound eager.

"Good. Meet me at headquarters no later than 6:30 a.m. If you're late, I'm not waiting on you."

The customer, who had observed me on the phone from a distance, said, "That must have been important. You look excited." I smiled and did not reply.

Shortly after the appointed hour on Monday morning I was in an unmarked police cruiser heading out of Savannah. Pete was at the wheel and mentioned that we'd be pulling off the expressway for a few minutes to pick up Jack Garrett. "He's been a tremendous help and inspiration to me over the years, and I thought he'd want to be there for this one." Once Jack was settled in, Pete continued, "I owe you guys an apology. I told you I'd keep you updated, but I've been so damned busy I just haven't had time. Let me give you the latest from the crime lab.

"The autopsy on Wiggins was interesting. He was shot three times. There was a deep soft tissue wound in his right neck. The bullet passed through, but in the process nicked his carotid artery, so it wouldn't have stopped him but he would have been bleeding heavily. The two other bullets hit his upper chest but didn't exit, so they were both recovered. They clipped some of the blood vessels in that area—they told me the names, but I can't remember them. Anyway, it's pretty certain any one of the three shots would have been fatal, unless he had immediate access to medical attention." Pete paused to pass an eighteen-wheeler. "Now, here's the important part. The barrel markings on the two slugs matched the rifling from the barrel of the Glock. And since the Glock belonged to Dr. Davis, he's got a lot of explaining to do. The bit about it being stolen was probably a coverup. And from our perspective, that finding made getting the search warrant a piece of cake. The judge didn't argue with us for one minute."

The green and white sign for Exit 84 led us to what had become a spontaneous roadside parking lot for crime lab and law enforcement vehicles, all awaiting the call from Savannah that the warrant had been served. We parked and Pete introduced Jack us to Kent Kitchens, the Toombs County sheriff. "As soon as I get the call, we're good to go, but off the record, there's a little drama that's probably gonna happen," the sheriff explained. "For several years, really since the Davis girl went missing, Dr. Davis has paid Billy Barlow, one of our retired deputies, to keep an eye on his property. Now, between us, Billy has been suspicious of things and keeps wondering why the doctor is so touchy about his farmhouse. But as Billy said, 'I'm retired, I could use the money, and he pays me well,' so he's been checking on things. We suspect that the first thing Davis will do is call Billy and see if he can stop or delay us. I talked to Billy about that, and he reminded me that the doctor had put out cameras everywhere around the place that he can see from an app on his phone. So, when we get there, Billy's probably going to be blocking the drive with his car. I'll get out and speak with him like we're having an argument, but we're just gonna be acting for the cameras since they can't hear what we're saying. And Billy is going to pretend to get angry but let us in because of the warrant. At least he'll get his check from Davis. Billy was with the department for many years. Retirement don't pay well. I owe him the favor." At that moment, the sheriff's cell buzzed. He answered, said "Good," and then turned to the waiting officers. "Warrant's delivered; let's go."

Like the cavalry going into battle, the parade of patrol cars and crime scene vans headed south toward the Davis farmhouse. As we were pulling away, Pete Marsh commented, "I suspect we'll see Dr. Davis himself arrive before too long...."

CHAPTER 37

Sheriff Kitchens was correct. As the caravan neared the Davis farm, a familiar-looking ancient pickup blocked the driveway at the turnoff from the dirt road. Billy Barlow, his arms crossed over his chest and a defiant look on his face, leaned against the hood. The sheriff, who had been leading the line of vehicles, stopped, got out of his patrol car and seemed to engage in a heated conversation with Barlow, who waved his arms and pointed to the farmhouse. The sheriff, appearing agitated, thrust the paper near Barlow's face, pointing at something on it. The older man appeared to read it, and with evident reluctance allowed the vehicles to proceed up the drive.

Parking in front of the house, the deputies fanned out to be certain that no one else was on the premises. Pete Marsh, Jack Garrett and I waited by our car, chatting with the sheriff while the crime scene techs, assisted by several Toombs County deputies, gained access to the interior of the house. "Are you going to have to make a forced entry?" Jack asked.

"Nah, not since the crime lab discovered there was an easier way than smashing their way in. Watch," the sheriff said, pointing to the front porch door. A twenty-someish blonde female tech kneeled in front of the door, peering at the double locks, one in the doorknob and a second separate deadbolt above. Glancing at his wristwatch, the sheriff said, "I'm guessing she'll be inside in less than ten minutes." Having assessed the situation, the tech fished in a folding pouch and retrieved two slim slivers of metal. "Looks like all she's going to need is a rake and a tension tool," he observed. Six and a half minutes later both locks were sprung and the door open. Three crime scene specialists, one of whom was carrying a camera, entered the house and began their work.

"This going to take a good while," Pete said. "They'll let us know if they find something." We picked a spot and sat on the earth while the techs came and went. A deputy brought by a large thermos of black coffee which we drank from paper cups.

The sheriff, who had known Peter Davis's father before his death, said he would be appalled at the scene we were viewing. "He was a good man, hardworking, and a great doctor. He'd pulled himself up by his own bootstraps, and cared so much about his family, always wanting the best for them. Now his daughter's dead—murdered—and his son, well...." He was interrupted by one of the crime techs beckoning to us from the porch of the house. "Looks like they've got something for us," he said.

We hurried over toward the house. "What have you found?" the sheriff asked.

"Blood, a lot of it. Looks like someone tried to clean it up, but with luminol it lights up like a Christmas tree."

"Where at?"

"The larger bedroom. Come in and I'll show you."

The interior of the house was comfortably furnished for relaxation and entertainment, certainly not as it must have been when it was the center of a small family farm. The bedroom where the blood was found was in the front part of structure, a moderate sized room with a double bed, dresser and private bath. A large fireplace was located on one wall. Windows on either side looked out on the surrounding pasture. The tech pointed to a spot on one side of the bed where a soft blue glow of the luminol indicated the presence of dried blood. "You can see the blood on the floor here, along with signs of where someone tried to clean it up. That's one patch. And over here," he said, pointing to an area adjacent to the fireplace, "is another smaller patch of blood, and again with indications that there was an effort to remove it. They couldn't get it all, though. This old wooden floor is full of small cracks and crevices, and that's what we're seeing."

"That's quite a bit," the sheriff said. "Musta been a hell of a fight."

"We're really just getting started here," the tech said, "but I thought you'd want to know right away that we'd found something that appears significant. And there's more. Look here," he said, pointing at a small defect in the casing around the bedroom entry door. "That looks like a bullet hole. We're going to have to tear some things out to see if....." He suddenly stopped at the sound of shouting from the direction of the front porch.

"Let me in, dammit! This is my house and you have no right to be here."

"Looks like Dr. Davis has arrived. I thought he would have been here earlier," the sheriff observed. We all headed toward the porch.

Sheriff Kennedy took the lead; we followed behind. "Dr. Davis, how are you this morning?" His tone was pleasant but neutral.

"I'm mad as hell. What is all this about? You're invading my property, conducting an illegal fishing expedition and...."

"You were duly served with the warrant earlier this morning."

"And I would have been here sooner, but I had to call my lawyer. He couldn't get away to come with me, but you'll hear from him for sure. There's no basis for the warrant and...." He suddenly stopped, spying me as I lingered in the doorway. "You!" he screamed, pointing at me.

"He's behind this one hundred percent. And my attorney...."

The sheriff waved his hands. "There are a few things you might not be aware of, Dr. Davis." The doctor remained silent. "You probably did not know that the crime lab searched again near the site where your sister's body was found. They discovered a second body, a man they've identified as Brandon Wiggins. And in the hole with him were two pistols, one of which belonged to you at one time, so...."

Davis blanched and looked for a brief moment like he might collapse. "How did you...? Why did you...?" he stammered, looking for words.

"Good detective work, I'd say," the sheriff replied.

"I'm leaving then," Davis said, having regained some of his composure. "But you will hear from my attorney, and I can guarantee you that this illegal search will not only be thrown out, it will be the basis of a multimillion-dollar lawsuit against whoever is behind it, as well as you personally, Kennedy."

"That's a risk I'm willing to take," the sheriff replied confidently. "But could I ask you to calmly leave the premises? Otherwise I will have to have my deputies detain you until the crime lab is finished with its work."

Without replying Davis stormed off the porch, hopped into his BMW and flew out of the drive in a cloud of dust. "Not a happy camper," Jack Garrett observed dryly.

Pete Marsh suggested we consider returning to Savannah. "If my guess is correct, I think the crew has discovered things that will give us enough to take this case to a grand jury for indictment. I'm going to assume the blood was Wiggins's. That doesn't explain the details about Mindy's death, but I believe they're just getting started with their work, and in any case, it's going to be a week or two before they get the basic analysis done."

"Can they do DNA testing on the blood?" I asked.

"Maybe," Pete replied. "From what I've been told, it depends on several factors. Someone tried to clean the blood up, and that could have damaged the DNA. And the blood's been there for several years. That might be a problem. We'll have to wait and see, I guess." We were mostly silent on the ride back to Savannah, thinking, wondering what would come next.

I was back at work at the gallery the next morning, silently marveling at the tranquility of rooms filled with art when only twenty-four hours earlier I had been at what appeared to be the blood-soaked scene of a violent murder. Shortly before ten o'clock, Jessica barged into my office, appearing frightened. "There's a man out there who says he's been sent to deliver a message to you. He looks kinda rough."

I walked out to see a large-framed man wearing blue jeans and an open-necked shirt. His size alone made him appear menacing. "Can I help you?" I asked.

"Yeah. You Mr. O'Toole?"

"I am."

"I'm from the law firm of Nippy Newsome. He wanted me to give you this." He handed me an envelope.

"Thank you. Anything else?"

"Yeah. I'm supposed to tell you to read that carefully, and to keep your nose out of other people's business." Despite the man's large cranium, he didn't appear to be especially bright.

"And if I don't?"

"Bad things gonna happen, I guess. I'm just delivering the message."

I thanked him and sent him on his way.

Jessica had been hovering behind me and heard the exchange. "He was threatening you, John." She sounded upset.

"Yes, it would be difficult not to pick up on that," I said, grinning. "Do you know Nippy Newsome?"

"No."

"He's a billboard lawyer, a lot of bluster and BS, that kind of thing, hoping to scare whoever his client is up against. But Newsome has a reputation among the legal community of backing down pretty quickly if the intimidation gambit doesn't work. Don't know why Davis is focusing on me, but he's wasting his time. At this point the police are running things and it looks like they're building a good case."

CHAPTER 38

For the remainder of the week and for most of the following, I heard nothing. On Friday of that second week, Pete Marsh called. "A lot has been going on, and I've got some updates for you. First, the lab was able to identify the small blood stain in the Davis cabin as Mindy's based on DNA. They were able to extract some DNA from the large stain, too, but haven't had any luck identifying it. It belonged to a male, and they still believe it's Brandon Wiggins. But there are problems: he was an only child, his parents are uncooperative and refuse to give a sample of their DNA to compare with the sample from the farmhouse, and Brandon and his wife had no children. And if that's not enough, the wife is acting like the parents, refusing to let the lab folks see if they can find a sample of his DNA at his house. They're still working on it and hope to come up with a definite answer before any trial.

"And speaking of a trial, the DA for the Toombs County circuit has a grand jury impaneled and hopes to present the case to them in the next couple of weeks. He's going to try to indict Peter Davis, Jr. for both the murders of Brandon and Mindy, but I believe he's going to have problems convincing the panel to bring an indictment for either one or both murders. Most importantly, it's a circumstantial case based on evidence alone. Any criminal defense attorney would point out that without the DNA confirmation, we don't have a definite ID for the body the state says is Brandon's, not to mention a motive for killing Mindy, his own sister. Also, Peter was living in Cleveland at the time, and might argue he wasn't within 500 miles of the cabin when the killings took place. What bothers me the most, and should bother the DA, is that we are reasonably certain that even if Peter did the killings, something had to happen, some blowup that led to the violence. And on top of that, he had to have some assistance. How else did Mindy's car and Brandon's pickup get moved? Failing to explain either of those questions to a jury could easily get him off the hook, and that's assuming he gets indicted and the case goes to trial."

An idea occurred to me. If one of the other individuals whom we assumed were there could be somehow prodded into voluntarily testifying, the pieces would all fall into place. I remembered something from my childhood. "Have you thought about trying to shake some vines to scare out a witness?" I asked.

"What are you talking about?"

"Back when I was a little kid—maybe twelve or thirteen—I used to go squirrel hunting with my grandfather. We'd get out in the woods and find a big tree with a squirrel nest up in it. We'd sit there and wait quietly for a squirrel to come along. And if one didn't, my granddad would send me out to shake one of the vines running up the tree and flush out a squirrel or two. We'd bring 'em home for my grandmother to fix for supper—'bushy-tailed rats'—she called them. It was one of those lessons you learn and pass on. My granddad's dad had taken him squirrel hunting and he thought the experience should be part of every boy's childhood."

There was silence at the other end of the line, then, "John, what the hell does that have to do with this case? We're talking getting indictments for a couple of murders and you're talking about squirrel hunting. What have you been smoking?"

"Hey, take it easy, Pete. Think about it. We are pretty sure Davis didn't act alone. If the way we see the killings is correct, there was at least one—maybe two—other people there. Brandon's truck had to be moved to the southern part of the county. Mindy's car had to be returned to Savannah. Whoever drove them needed to get back home and someone had to take them. It was probably done at night to avoid being seen. If, say, Davis were indicted for one or both murders and the case against him looked strong, he could try to plea-bargain his side of the case by fingering his accomplices. On the other side of the coin, if one of the accomplices hears that the case is going before a grand jury and realizes the chances of the doctor trying to save his own skin by blaming them, they might just suddenly feel like they could come out better if they volunteered to tell 'the truth' to the grand jury with some story about Peter doing the killings and threatening to kill them, too, if they reported it. See what I mean?"

Pete was silent for a moment. "Complicated, but you may have a point. How would you handle it?"

"I'd think there are issues of confidentiality, and we'd have to be very careful. You could ask a cooperative reporter to do an interview with the DA inquiring about progress on the case. The reporter would then do a news report with some headline like "District Attorney Plans to Present Evidence to Grand Jury," and specifically saying he feels he has a very strong case and is certain there will be indictments—use the plural—and at the same time calling for input from the public if anyone has additional information. Get it in print, on radio and TV, on social media, so the maximum number of people have the potential to see it. That's shaking the vine. It could flush out a few squirrels."

Again, there was a brief silence. Then Pete said, "Thinking outside of the box, but I like it."

A week later the news broke that the district attorney for the Toombs County circuit revealed to a reporter that based on newly discovered evidence—he was presumably referring to the raid on the Davis farmhouse—he was confident that indictments in the murder of Mary Nelle Davis would be issued soon. The story rated a brief segment on the regional news stations, a number follow-up articles in the small town and big city print editions, was featured on the online news feeds, and was posted and shared from several Facebook accounts. Pete texted, "We've shaken the vines. Waiting now for the squirrels to poke their heads out." Three days later, he texted again, this time with the cryptic, "Bingo! Bagged our game. We'll see how this goes."

CHAPTER 39

I learned most of the details later, but as events had evolved, within forty-eight hours of the time the story on the pending indictments became public, the Toombs County District Attorney received a call from Walter Bingham, a criminal defense attorney with a large and well-respected Atlanta law firm. Bingham said he had been contacted by, and soon met with, an unnamed individual whom he stated was present at the scene of the crimes, and would be willing to testify to a grand jury and subsequently in court "under a certain set of conditions." He stated that to the best of his knowledge, his client had not been considered as having any direct involvement in the case, but had the misfortune of being there at the time of the murders. Using neutral pronouns to avoid giving away their gender, he stated the client had been threatened by someone—again, no name or demographics were given—and feared for their life. Bingham said this person's motivation for their willingness to testify was to avoid being charged as an accessory, or worse, accomplice. He stated his client was offering testimony that would provide the details of the crimes that undoubtedly would lead to the conviction of the guilty parties, but in exchange would like assurance that they themselves would avoid prosecution. It was a sudden and stunning revelation.

Although grand jury rules and protocols vary from state to state, the purpose is the same, the presentation of an alleged set of facts to an impartial body of jurors whose sole duty is to decide whether the evidence establishes "probable cause" that the accused person or persons have committed a crime. If so, that leads to an indictment and arrest of the accused. Grand jury presentations and deliberations are considered secret, including the identity of witnesses. Attorneys for the accused are not present, cross-examination of witnesses is not allowed and no transcript of the proceedings is kept.

After a preliminary agreement in principle was reached with the district attorney, Bingham revealed the name of his client, Anna Wiggins, the widow of Brandon. She underwent two full days of questioning by police investigators led by Pete Marsh, by members of the district attorney's staff, and by the DA himself. Having reached the conclusion that her account was valid and would, in Pete's words, "give us all we'll need for an indictment," she was scheduled for a presentation to the grand jury. Her testimony lasted some six and a half hours over a two-day period.

Anna Everett Wiggins was a few years younger than her late husband Brandon. They had originally met and been involved when both were students at the University of Georgia. Though not from Vidalia, she took a teaching position at the middle school there on graduation. Brandon was beginning his forestry career. They rekindled their relationship, and were soon married. It did not take long for Anna to become suspicious of Brandon's fidelity. She suspected him several times of being involved with other women, and on one occasion surprised him at the apartment of a girl he'd been seeing. She considered a divorce, but they both went to counseling and "worked things out," as she termed it. Over the year and a half before his death, Anna became aware that Brandon had fallen back to his old ways. She was torn between divorce, which she did not want, or waiting things out, thinking perhaps this was a phase Brandon was going through. In part, she blamed herself, suspecting their inability to conceive a child may have contributed to his infidelity. Finally, and without consulting anyone, she decided to divorce him. Knowing he would fight such a move, she set out to gather such overwhelming evidence against him that his contesting a divorce would be impossible and a jury would award her a large settlement for sticking with him as long as she had. Or so she believed.

Anna obtained and placed a tracking device in Brandon's truck. This was monitored via the internet and allowed her to see and make a record of his whereabouts, especially when she said he was acting "suspicious." He did indeed enjoy overnight fishing trips to the river, but on multiple occasions he spent the night elsewhere instead. Soon a pattern emerged. On a regular and frequent basis he appeared to be seeing Mindy Davis, usually meeting her at the Davis farmhouse and occasionally spending the night with her there or at her apartment in Savannah. And to her surprise, Anna found he was seeing someone else as well, the former Carole Marie Hastings, Brandon's college girlfriend and now wife of Dr. Peter Davis. Carole was living in Cleveland at the time, but visited her parents in Vidalia at least monthly. She and Brandon would see each other when she was in town.

The fateful weekend of Brandon's and Mindy's murders began with Brandon announcing to his wife that he planned to go fishing in the Altamaha, with his usual pattern of spending Saturday night there and returning about midday on Sunday after a morning on the river. She suspected he had other plans. By just after noon on Saturday, it was evident from the GPS device in his truck that he was at Mindy's farmhouse. She doubted he had any plans for fishing as the river was nearly twenty-five miles away at the other end of the county. "I got mad," she told the grand jury. "I knew what he was doing, but

I tried to calm down, to ignore it, to think that soon he'll realize we have a good marriage and will stop all this. But the more I thought about it, the madder I became. I didn't want to show up and confront him again—that would just make things worse. And maybe it wasn't Brandon, maybe it was that Davis girl; she was working in some strip club in Savannah. Maybe she was just after him for his money, or just a good time—I didn't know. I knew I had to do something, but something different. I knew Mindy's mother. I'd met her at church, and she seemed like a fine lady, so I decided to just show up at her house, tell her what was going on, and ask her to go to the farmhouse with me. Possibly having her mother show up and catch her with someone else's husband would convince Mindy to back off. And if we went through with the divorce and it got ugly, I could call her as a witness for my side. So I looked up Mrs. Davis's address, got in my car and headed to her house."

On arriving at the Davis residence, Anna noticed another car in the front driveway but didn't think anything of it. She ran the doorbell on the front porch and was greeted at the door by Mrs. Davis, who seemed surprised at her visit, but invited her in. Just as they were entering the family room at the rear of the house, Mrs. Davis said, "I don't know if you've met my son, Dr. Peter Davis, and his wife, Carole?" Anna had not met her son, but immediately recognized Carole, the other woman that her husband seemed to be involved with.

"I had to think quickly," Anna told the jury. "I had come to discuss the situation with Mindy's mother, but here I was in the room with her brother and my husband's other mistress. I didn't know if Peter—that's Dr. Davis—knew about his wife and Brandon, but it didn't matter. Carole looked frightened. She knew I was her boyfriend's wife, and seemed terrified that

I was about to tell her husband about Brandon. I figured she'd go along with things—anything to keep from bringing up her relationship with him.

"We all sat down. Mrs. Davis offered me coffee. I declined. There was this awkward silence. She explained that Peter and Carole were visiting for the weekend. They'd flown down to Atlanta and rented a car. Finally Mrs. Davis said, 'What can we do for you this fine day?' and I replied 'You—all of you—can help me stop my husband and Mindy from seeing each other. They've been having an affair for a long time and it's ruining my marriage.'

"Mrs. Davis turned pale. Peter frowned and became red-faced, a large vein popped up on his forehead like he was going to explode. Carole kinda sunk into the chair, looking like someone was going to hit her. I waited for someone to say something."

Mrs. Davis broke the silence saying, "I am—no, we are—aware of my daughter's lifestyle. It's an embarrassment to us all. I have begged and pleaded with her to stop, to turn her life over to Jesus, but she won't listen. Oh, she's been good to me, helping out since her father passed away, but still.... It's brought shame to the family name." Peter said nothing, still red-faced and obviously angry. Carole appeared to have shrunk in size, still frightened that her secrets would be revealed.

"Mrs. Davis," Anna continued, "I don't know exactly what I should ask you to do, but could you possibly talk with Mindy, tell her she's ruining my marriage. And don't think I'm putting all the blame on her—it takes two, I know. I have a feeling that my husband may be ruining other marriages as well, but I have no control over him...." Anna commented that she looked at Carole as she spoke and realized that "she knew that I knew."

Peter Davis, who had said nothing to this point, asked, "Where are Mindy and your husband now?"

"At Mindy's farmhouse, up in the north part of the county. I have a GPS tracker in Brandon's truck."

"Let's go," he said, standing up.

"Who?" his mother asked. "And why?"

"All of us—including you, Anna," Peter said. "We need to catch them, embarrass them, confront them with what their selfishness is doing to all of us, to our families, to our reputations....". Carole put her hands over her face. "Come on, Carole. I want you to go, too." He grabbed her hand and headed toward their car parked in the front drive. Mrs. Davis and Anna followed.

CHAPTER 40

The Davis family took Peter's rental car. Peter drove, with Mrs. Davis in the front and Carole in the back seat, no doubt fearful of how a confrontation between her husband, her lover, her lover's wife, her lover's other mistress, and her mother-in-law might play out. Anna followed in her own car, the same set of concerns coursing through her thoughts. It was mid-afternoon as the two vehicles pulled into the driveway of the farmhouse. Without waiting for his mother or wife, Peter leapt out of the car and bounded up the front steps, trying the door handle without knocking. It appeared to be locked. Reaching in his pocket he pulled out a set of keys and began searching for the correct one. Meanwhile Mrs. Davis, Carole and Anna had exited their cars and approached the steps. "What are you going to do, Peter?" his mother demanded.

"I'm going to face down this bastard," he said in a low voice. Finding the right key, he turned it in both locks, then quietly eased open the door and slipped in, followed by the three women. The front room was empty. The door to the bedroom was closed, with the sound of music from inside reverberating through the walls. Walking carefully to avoid making a sound, Peter stepped over to a cupboard and eased open a large drawer. Reaching into what was apparently a hidden compartment, he extracted a small black automatic pistol which he then stuffed in his pocket. Glancing back at his mother, Carole and Anna, he suddenly flung the door open.

The interior of the room was flooded with dim light and music. Two figures could be seen entangled on the bed. The male, Brandon, sat up, clearly surprised. The female, Mindy, screamed and pulled up the sheets to cover herself. Brandon yelled, "Get the hell out of here!" while reaching over toward his pants which lay in a crumpled heap next to the bed. Mindy cowered, the sheets covering her face such that only her eyes were exposed.

"Who do you think…?" Brandon began, then stopped when he spied Anna peeking through the door. Ignoring his nakedness, he sprang out of bed, just as Peter was pulling the pistol out of his pocket. It had not been clear in the dimness of the room, but when Brandon reached out for his pants, he had grabbed his revolver which he now fired in Peter's direction. The bullet narrowly missed, striking the door casing next to Anna's head. Peter then fired back as Brandon lunged toward him, the bullet striking him in the flesh of his neck but not stopping his momentum. He tackled Peter, dropping his revolver in the process while knocking the pistol from Peter's hand. It skidded across the floor. The two men collapsed on the floor in a grappling mass of arms and legs and fists. As this was happening, Mindy, seeing her brother shoot Brandon, began screaming. Ignoring her own nakedness she leapt on top of Peter and Brandon, trying desperately to pull her brother away from her lover.

For a few seconds after the battle began, Mrs. Davis, Anna and Carole stood just inside the doorway, frozen with fear and shock. Then Mrs. Davis sprang into action like someone a fraction of her age. Bounding across the floor in two long steps she grabbed her daughter and dragged her away from the struggling men. Mindy fought back, stunning her mother with a fist to her jaw, knocking the older lady into the mantel of the fireplace. Mindy then leapt back into the fray, continuing her efforts to pull Peter away from Brandon.

Meanwhile, Mrs. Davis pulled herself up and again jerked her daughter off the men, throwing Mindy toward the fireplace area, where she herself had lain seconds before. In the process, Mindy's head struck the mantel shelf, temporarily stunning her. Seeing her chance, Mrs. Davis grabbed the fireplace poker and, swinging it like a golf club, struck her daughter across the right side of her face just below her eye. Mindy crumpled in a heap on the floor, blood flowing freely from the wound opened by the blow. With Brandon and Peter still struggling on the floor, Mrs. Davis sat on her now unconscious daughter's chest and began strangling her, screaming "You useless whore. You're the devil in the flesh and I'm going to kill you...." The sound of two quick gunshots stopped her mid-sentence. In the middle of the melee Peter had managed to reach his pistol, shooting Brandon twice in the chest.

The room was suddenly quiet.

As if awakened from a dream, Peter still lay on top of Brandon's now lifeless body, while Mindy lay motionless on the floor as blood poured from her wound, her visionless eyes staring off into space. For what seemed like an eternity, no one spoke. Then, in a hoarse voice, Mrs. Davis croaked, "Sweet Lord, what have we done?"

The world had changed for everyone in the room. Brandon and Mindy were dead. Peter and his mother were murderers. Anna and Carole were witnesses, if not accessories to the crimes. For the next hour they talked. In the heat of the discussion, Peter revealed that he had long suspected that his wife had been "seeing this Brandon guy," suggesting that discovering him with Mindy could be a motive for his murder. "Wasn't it enough to be married to a doctor, a high-dollar cardiologist, or did you want someone who spends his days in the woods and his weekends fishing?" Anna said she found that insulting, and that Brandon was a good man. Peter replied, "Maybe so, but he's now a dead man, and we're all on the hook for it unless we can come up with a plan."

The first suggestion—from Anna—was to burn the house, making it appear that Mindy and Brandon had died in the fire. Both Peter and his mother rejected that, Peter saying that the house and farm was about all he would inherit, and Mrs. Davis saying the farm represented their heritage and memories of the past she and her husband had struggled so desperately to overcome. Noting the boat in the back of Brandon's truck, one of the group suggested that it might be possible to make it appear that he drowned while fishing. Anna testified that she could not remember who came up with this idea. All agreed on that option and with it, returning Mindy's car to her apartment in Savannah so the search would be centered there. Peter volunteered to hide the bodies. He wasn't sure at the time how or where he would accomplish the task, but he thought he would most likely bury them in a place where they would never be found. That evening they would conceal the bodies and move both of the victims' vehicles to other locations. All four agreed to return the next morning to do a thorough cleanup of the crime scene in the house.

The district attorney, questioning Anna during her testimony before the grand jury, asked her specifically how Mrs. Davis and Peter had reacted to Mindy's death. She replied, "They seemed relieved, as if a thorn had been removed from their flesh, and far more concerned about the coverup than the killings." It was a damning statement that one grand juror—later and anonymously—said was the one thing all agreed on when deciding to indict Mrs. Daniel Peter Davis, Sr. and her son, Dr. Daniel Peter Davis, Jr., for the murders of Mary Nelle Davis and Brandon Wiggins.

The plan worked. The victims' vehicles were moved without detection, the farmhouse cleaned as much as possible, the evidence—clothes, the two pistols and so forth—buried with the bodies. Both Mindy and Brandon were declared missing, though as far as the world new, these tragic events, appearing to be unrelated and apparently occurring miles apart, were never connected by the original investigators.

Two days after Anna Wiggins's testimony before the Toombs County grand jury, the panel issued true bills indicting the Davis mother and son for the murders of Mindy and Brandon. Normally, such an indictment would be passed to members of law enforcement for the arrest of the suspects. The indictments, considered to be confidential until officially announced and the arrests made, were handed down on a Friday. The arrests of the Davises were planned for the following Monday.

On Saturday morning, the following day, Carole Davis, Peter's wife, noted that he received a phone call on his private cell phone. She did not hear the conversation, but saw him pacing back and forth by the pool in his yard as he talked. He seemed either annoyed or upset; she wasn't sure, but immediately on ending that call placed another. About an hour later Peter told Carole that he was going to drive over to Vidalia to visit with his mother, and planned to be home in time for supper. She said they could grill out if he liked; he said that sounded good. He kissed her and his two children and left.

Just before 5:00 p.m. that afternoon, several motorists on I-16 East observed a late model blue BMW 7-Series sedan traveling toward Savannah at a high rate of speed, estimated to be in excess of a hundred miles an hour. Three reliable witnesses reported that near Exit 132, Ash Branch Church Road, the vehicle appeared to veer off the expressway without braking, as if aiming itself at the concrete foundation that supported the overpass there. The high velocity impact destroyed the car, killing both occupants instantly. The victims were later identified as Dr. Daniel Peter Davis, Jr., a cardiologist from Savannah, and his mother, Mildred Wilford Davis, of Vidalia.

EPILOGUE

The victims' "tragic deaths" that occurred on Interstate 16 warranted prominent notice in the Savannah press as well as online in social media. Despite his relative youth, Dr. Davis was said to be "a pillar of the community" and a "valued member of the medical profession." His mother, Mildred, received equally fatuous accolades; only a few individuals knew of the indictments and the lurid tale that accompanied them. Although rumors circulated for some time, the district attorney revealed nothing and the records of the Toombs County grand jury remained sealed. As far as the public knew, the Davises perished with their reputations untarnished.

Carole Davis, Peter's wife, was never seriously considered for legal action despite her presence at the murder scene. She committed no punishable crime, and her marital status would likely prevent her from giving testimony against the others.

Anna Wiggins's situation was another matter. She had testified to the grand jury that someone suggested making her husband's death appear to be an accidental drowning. Unlike the remainder of her detailed testimony, however, she could not recall which one of the other three originally raised the idea. As it turned out, she and her husband had taken out a $1.5 million term life insurance policy on him a year or two earlier. The policy was for ten years, and carried a double-indemnity clause in the case of accidental death. Six weeks after his disappearance Anna filed to collect the three million dollars due from the policy. As might be expected, the insurance company balked at paying the policy limits. To begin with, her husband was "missing," not "deceased." Additionally, the fine print of the policy gave the company adequate time for "investigation" in such cases. It appeared that any payout, if it happened, could be delayed for years.

Anna, via an attorney, filed a petition with the local Superior Court to have Brandon declared dead. She was successful, and rather than litigate, the insurance carrier suggested an initial payment of $100,000, followed by annual payments thereafter over a period of twenty years, including interest on the remaining balance. She agreed to that, and by the time Brandon's body was discovered had received several hundred thousand dollars. When the news of the discovery of the body finally became public, Anna was sued by the insurance company for fraud, and was indicted, tried and convicted on the same charge, earning her several years in prison.

There were loose ends of course; there always are. One mystery was solved about three weeks after the Davises' death when Lauren Yates called and came by the gallery to drop off a flash drive containing the audio of the call to the tip line that implied Brandon Wiggins was Mindy's boyfriend. "They took forever to get this to me," Lauren complained. "I guess it doesn't really matter now, but I'm curious to see if you have any idea who made the call."

I slipped the drive into my computer and turned up the sound. The distinctive voice of Mildred Davis filled my office. It did not matter now, indeed, but at least we knew.

As to Jenna, who was in some way responsible for this entire saga, all was well. Saddened though she was, she learned the secret of her friend's death. "That's all I really wanted to know," she told me on several occasions. We had wasted a year of our lives discovering answers to questions we never wanted to ask. I was still in love with her, and now that our lives seemed to have reached a steady course and an even keel, I wanted once again to consider asking her to marry me.

I have a tendency to overthink things. In retrospect, my dramatic plans to ask Jenna to marry me while we were in Madrid were a total disaster. This time, if it happened, the request, the offer, would be more casual, perhaps even spontaneous. And I swore to myself that I would not devise carefully thought-out, detailed plans, the sort that had crashed my first attempt. Visiting the bank, I retrieved the diamond and sapphire ring in its red leather pouch from the safe deposit box, moving it instead to the small safe in my office at the gallery. I wanted to be ready when the moment presented itself.

Weeks passed; everything remained calm. The gallery sales continued to do well. The world seemed brighter. Mindy and all that had taken place were never mentioned in my conversations with Jenna. Once again I suggested that we spend a weekend away, perhaps in the inn we'd stayed at earlier in Beaufort. She seemed excited about the idea. I booked a long weekend, Thursday through Sunday. There was no agenda, just the two of us, walking, talking, dining, and sleeping together.

I thought perhaps this might be the time. Though I had no scripted plans as before, I still wanted to be prepared just in case I felt brave enough to bring up the subject of marriage. So, I'd taken the ring out of my office safe and hidden it again in my suitcase. Our Thursday together was beautiful, as were Friday and Saturday. We walked and talked, dined well, drank wine in moderation and generally reveled in each other's company.

For Saturday night, I made reservations at the small restaurant where we had dined on our earlier visit. The fine menu, great wine list and candlelight made for the perfect atmosphere.

We shared a vegan charcuterie board as an appetizer accompanied by a glass of Sancerre white, followed by duck breast for Jenna and a petite fillet with braised scallops for me, sharing a bottle of Los Vascos Chilean cabernet. Having eaten and drunk far more than usual, we both ordered coffee and made small talk. I was feeling the warm glow of the wine, there was no doubt of that. I slipped my hand in my pocket, touching the leather pouch holding the ring I planned to offer to Jenna. There was a moment of silence, which I broke with, "I love you."

Jenna smiled, reached across the table and placed her hand over mine. "I love you, too. I think you know that." She paused, then said. "But I think there's something we need to talk about." My body spontaneously tensed, fearful of what she was about to say. "Last year, that week we spent in Spain before all this came up about Mindy, those were some of the most wonderful days of my life. You know me. You know all about me, my failures, my sins, my sometimes weird moods, all that I am. And I come with baggage. I have a son, the product of one failed marriage. I was on drugs. I was working as a stripper, and worse...." Jenna reached up to dab a tear from her eye. "But knowing all that and knowing me better than anyone else ever could, you still tell me you love me. It's sometimes hard to understand...."

"Jenna...," I began. She held her finger to her lips, shushing me.

"When we were in Madrid that last day, I wanted so much to do something I am not supposed to do. I wanted to ask you to marry me. Yes, I know that's backwards, that the man asks the woman and all that, but we've never had a totally normal, routine white-bread relationship since we first met. I wanted so much to let you know how I feel, to tell you that I wanted to spend the rest of my life with you. And then, before I got the chance, that crazy painting was there, and a flood of memories, horrid memories, pushed everything else out of my head. You said you went to Dr. Martin's place. Did he show you the building behind his house?"

"Yes, but…."

"Please let me finish, John."

"So you saw his dioramas, drama stages really, based on the painting, *The Garden of Earthly Delights*?"

"I saw one. He said it was the middle panel, a vision of Paradise."

"But you didn't see the others, especially the construction he called Bosch's vision of Hell?"

"I didn't know there were others. It was a huge building and I suppose…."

"Martin was a pervert who tried to use his position as a professor to seduce innocent students by making them believe they were participating in some sort of art project. I was one of them. He wanted me to role-play—with him acting as the devil. I escaped before something terrible happened, but…, but Mindy didn't. I think that changed the rest of her life. She felt dirty, used, worthless. So after that nothing else really seemed to matter. Her life went downhill from there."

"Jenna…," I started but again she signaled me to remain silent. I grasped the pouch in my pocket, thinking this might be the right time.

"Please let me finish, John. I love you, and I want to marry you. But not now, not until I get my head screwed back on correctly. I don't want something to happen. I don't want to disappoint you—or me. I need some time before we take things any further. That doesn't mean that our relationship needs to change, but rather I need to convince myself that I'm worthy of your love and trust. Please understand. You mean everything to me."

I pushed the pouch with the ring deeper into my pocket and reached out for Jenna's hand. "We have all the time in the world, Jenna. We'll take it slow and easy."

[THE END]

ACKNOWLEDGMENTS

I am most appreciative for the input and suggestions from my "readers" of this latest John Wesley O'Toole novel. Perhaps needless to say, this is a work of fiction. All characters and situations are entirely products of the mind of the author. With that said, to add a sense of verisimilitude the events often take place in actual locations, including, for example, the city of Savannah and the surrounding areas of south Georgia. I want to thank as well the staff of Mercer University Press for their support and encouragement with this and my other recent published works.